ABOUT THIS BOOK

From the heat of summertime Italy to the icy winter of upstate New York, the stories in this collection feature one common element: strong woman who stand up and face their fears.

Whether to protect themselves or loved ones, to fight injustice and right a wrong, they find ways to prevail.

Includes the story "The Scent of Amber and Vanilla," which was called a "nail-biter" by Publisher's Weekly and received an honorable mention in The Year's Best Crime & Mystery 2016.

Praise for Dayle A. Dermatis

"Dermatis has a love of lush language...."

— Tangent Online

VOICES CARRY
Dayle A. Dermatis

Ebook edition published 2024 by Soul's Road Press

This is a work of fiction. Names, characters, places, and events are either the product of the author's imagination or are used fictitiously, and any resemblance to actual persons, living or dead, business establishments, events, or locales is entirely coincidental.

"The Florentine Exchange" was originally published in *Fiction River: Spies*, WMG Publishing, 2018.
"Bothering With the Details" was originally published in *Alfred Hitchcock's Mystery Magazine*, 2018.
"Why Don't You Make Gingerbread?" originally appeared in *Bloody Christmas: A Holiday Anthology*, WMG Publishing, 2020.
"Stupid Games" was originally published by Soul's Road Press, 2020.
"Girl With a Mission" was originally published in *Fiction River: Hard Choices*, WMG Publishing, 2018.
"Voices Carry" was originally published in *Snowbound: Best New England Crime Stories 2017*, Level Best Books, 2017.
"Clap Your Hands if You Believe" was originally published by Soul's Road Press, 2015.
"Women Who Love Dogs" was originally published in *Me Too Short Stories*, Level Best Books, 2019.
"Pirate Pete's" was originally published in *Alfred Hitchcock's Mystery Magazine*, 2019.
"The Scent of Amber and Vanilla" was originally published in *Fiction River: Pulse Pounders*, WMG Publishing, 2015.

ISBN 978-1-946462-16-9

Inquiries should be addressed to
Soul's Road Press
info@soulsroadpress.com
http://www.soulsroadpress.com

VOICES CARRY

and Other Stories of Women and Crime

DAYLE A. DERMATIS

SOUL'S
ROAD
PRESS

CONTENTS

Libby normally didn't mind the narrow, five-story staircase that spiraled up to their apartment at the top of the 15th-century former monastery, because the lack of elevator was a small price to pay for living in Florence, Italy—and living her dream job in covert operations.

She minded the lack of air conditioning, however, especially on days like this: hot, stuffy, breezeless, with only a few high clouds that did nothing to break the sun's spell. The wooden stair treads dipped and angled, worn by centuries of footfalls; if she didn't step carefully, she'd trip. The only minor plus was that the building smelled of tomato sauce and oregano and onions—a vast improvement from the odor of exhaust trapped in the narrow streets outside.

By the time she'd lugged the heavy bag of clean laundry up the stairs, she was sticky with humidity and ready to peel off her damp clothes and throw them right into the bag. The problem with going to a launderette was you couldn't be naked while you washed your clothes.

She unlocked the door and shoved it with her shoulder—

the wood always swelled and the upper right corner stuck—and stumbled inside.

The studio apartment was long and narrow, with unadorned white walls, tall enough that there was room for a loft at one end. You could stand beneath the loft, but only sit upright, not stand, when you were up there. The loft had the only window, so they'd dragged the mattresses up there to sleep, grateful for the cooler night air.

She assumed Antonia had already left for her assignment, but then she heard the toilet flush. The bathroom had been added at a later time, a boxy corner room with a ceiling as high as the loft floor, creating a flat surface above, where they'd shoved suitcases and other things they didn't use regularly. From the loft, you had a view of the dust in the corners.

When Antonia emerged, Libby took in the details in one glance, just as she'd been trained: The fact that Antonia was wearing cut-off grey sweatpants and a red tank top when she should have been dressed for the cocktail reception at which she was assigned to do a data exchange. The fact that Antonia was barefoot, hopping on her right foot. The fact that an Ace bandage figure-eighted around her left ankle and foot.

Antonia—tiny, ashy-blond, and surprisingly unassuming when she was bare-faced and uncoiffed—grimaced. She hopped the few feet to the broken-springed loveseat and collapsed into it sideways, propping her leg up on the far arm.

"What happened?" Libby asked, dropping the laundry on the wooden straight chair that served as a dining chair, desk chair, and the only other seating in the apartment.

"My own stupidity," Antonia said. "You'll have to go to the embassy event instead. It's a simple exchange. You're ready for it." She glanced at her watch. "How soon can you leave?"

Soon enough, because that was the job. Libby had learned how to shower, dress, do makeup and hair in record time. She didn't wash her hair, just rinsed the sweat off her body under the shower nozzle that stuck out of the bathroom wall, no curtain or surround, one of those weird Italian things she'd grown used to, along with no washcloths and the disturbingly frequent public toilets without seats.

She was here largely as backup for Antonia, a more seasoned agent, and to learn from her. This would be her first solo assignment.

The flurry in her stomach wasn't nerves. Like Antonia had said, it was a simple exchange. She already knew who her contact was; Antonia had gone over that with her as a training exercise. She was finally getting to *do* something that was real, not a test, not a simulation.

She twisted her hair up into an artfully messy knot, the dampness making it easier to style, actually. Long and dyed dark brown, so she didn't stand out. Italian men noticed blonds, fawned over redheads. They commented on her height, five-foot-ten in bare feet (and nobody went barefoot in Italy), but there was little she could do about that except not wear the sky-high heels so fashionable nowadays. Easier to run, maneuver, fight if it came to that, in lower heels anyway.

Before Antonia zipped her into her cocktail dress, a sleek dark red number with a plunging neckline, Libby knelt in the bathroom, pulled out the plastic tub of cleaning supplies under the sink, pried up the false bottom in the cabinet, and opened the small, flat safe beneath.

She grabbed the ID she'd need—the one naming her as the daughter of a diplomat, just the type of person who'd be attending one of these parties—and the tiny thumb drive she'd be passing on to her contact. The drive was smaller than her thumbnail, no more than the part that inserted into a computer and the cover to protect it.

A quick glance in the mirror. Hair good, makeup good. A

sedate strand of pearls around her neck, with complementary pearl-and-gold earrings and pin.

Then it was quickly back down the wooden spiral staircase, all five stories, the click of her heels echoing.

Late afternoon sun slanted down the narrow street, turning the sandstone walls to gold and the terracotta roofs to burnished flame. As the blissfully air conditioned taxi pulled into a wider street, she could see the sky cast in shades of butter and salmon, a sight that thrilled her every evening.

She settled back against the seat and opened her purse. It had room for a slim wallet and her passport, lipstick and powder and emergency tampon, and her phone...as well as a secret compartment for her gun. She dipped into the main section to grab the thumb drive, intending to transfer it to the private compartment, but came up with a few coins and *two* thumb drives.

Two identical thumb drives.

She'd washed a few of Antonia's clothes at the launderette along with her own, and when she'd checked the pockets of one pair of slacks, she'd dumped the loose change into her purse. Apparently there had been a tiny thumb drive as well, jumbled with the coins.

She examined both drives. Same brand, size; both black. No way to tell them apart unless she looked at the contents of each.

And that wasn't something she could do in the cab.

Antonia waited a full five minutes after Libby's departure, patiently counting the seconds and minutes, just to make sure Libby didn't run back because she'd forgotten something. Antonia didn't expect that. Libby was at the very least conscientious, and at most borderline obsessive; she rarely forgot anything.

She was just young, naïve, and easily manipulated.

Antonia lounged on the sagging loveseat, still and sure, and when the five minutes were up, she sat up and stripped the Ace bandage from her perfectly fine ankle.

Libby would exchange the fake thumb drive with her contact, and Antonia would pass on the real one to someone who was willing to pay a hell of a lot more money than Antonia's meager salary.

She hadn't been expecting glitz and glamor, sure, but she also hadn't expected to be dumped in a shitty box of an apartment that felt like a sauna or to be expected to act as an errand girl.

She was done. Beyond done.

She headed to the bathroom, stripping out of her shorts and tank top on the way, leaving them where they fell, and dug down to the safe beneath the sink. She grabbed her various passports—she'd dispose of the government-issued ones later, keep only the one she'd had made—and the stacks of cash from all over the world, more than enough to get her out of the country.

A few steps across the room and she was at her wardrobe, a prefab, rickety thing tucked under the loft. She'd cultivated a habit of being messy, of scattering things around, to keep Libby from noticing things out of place. Habits were deadly in this business. So instead of putting the clothes she planned to wear somewhere obvious, such as laid out or hung at the front of the wardrobe, she'd tossed them in the bottom of the wardrobe with a few other random items, an ever-changing mishmash.

But the pale pink, three-quarter-sleeve shirt and the oatmeal-colored wide-legged linen pants were gone. The bras, the scarf, the jumble of shoes was still there, but no outfit.

Antonia stared, stunned, for a moment before whirling to scan the rest of the room. When her gaze hit the mesh laundry bag Libby had dropped on the chair by the door, she muttered a few choice curse words under her breath.

When Libby had said she was going to do laundry and did Antonia want her to throw any of her things in, Antonia had called out from the bathroom, where she'd been showering, to grab whatever was lying around—figuring Libby would pick up the items on the bed, draped over the chair, kicked in the corner. She'd never thought Libby would look in the wardrobe for dirty laundry.

But Libby was precise, thorough.

Antonia had underestimated Libby, and that was her own damn fault.

She upended the laundry bag onto Libby's bed, dumping the carefully folded clothes into a jumbled heap, and pawed through. Found her slacks.

The pockets were empty.

Antonia threw the slacks across the room.

Then she stood stock still, took in a low, slow, deep breath, and composed herself.

She had to think, make a plan. Stay focused.

Libby had both drives. The question was, did she realize it? Probably. Did she know what was on each drive? She wouldn't know which one to exchange otherwise.

Libby followed rules. Her job was to deliver the correct drive. She'd do everything possible to complete that job.

So, Antonia had to get to Libby before Libby exchanged the drive Antonia needed.

Antonia went back to the wardrobe and yanked out a new outfit.

IN ITALIAN, LIBBY ASKED THE DRIVER FOR A NEW destination: the Santa Maria Novella station, Florence's train hub. She paid him in cash, with a nice but unmemorable tip, and went inside.

The last of the sunlight streamed through the panes of glass that made up the roof and a sloping wall that reached the top of the ticket counters, dappling the heads of the travelers. A busy time of day, which was good—everyone was focused on their destination, on catching their train or getting outside to continue on their way, and not focused on each other. Beneath the hum of conversation, Libby's heels clicked on the floor of long stripes of veined marble, alternating off-white and dusty rose.

Past the people smelling of perfume and aftershave and body odor, past the ticket booths and machines, past the shops selling sandwiches and coffee and last-minute travel wares and gifts, to the storage room with its walls of lockers, a place for day tourists to store their travel gear.

From one of the lockers, Libby pulled a shopping bag, red with an understated gold logo, from a high-end, expensive boutique. The kind that ladies of leisure all over the city carried on a day of browsing; the kind nobody would look twice at. Her emergency stash.

She locked the locker, pocketed the key. She'd toss it somewhere after she wiped it down, just to be safe.

Back outside, where the sun hovered on the horizon, casting long shadows, she hailed another blessedly air-conditioned taxi to take her to the cocktail party.

She sat in the back behind the passenger seat; the driver would have to turn his head to see her, not just glance in his mirror. Holding her items below his sightline, she pulled a small device, which looked like an external phone battery, from the shopping bag and inserted one end into her phone. In the other, she slipped one of the thumb drives.

Although her phone didn't have all the functionality of a computer, it did have some extra capabilities—thanks to her employer—that would allow her to get a general sense of what was on the two drives.

It was easy to tell the difference, at least. The false drive initially looked as though it contained the correct information, but the files were too small.

Then again, the operative slated to receive the drive wouldn't have the chance to look at it until well after the exchange had been made, and by then it would have been too late.

Libby touched her teeth to her lower lip; not actively chewing on it, though, which would have marred her lipstick.

Did Antonia have a separate job, one she hadn't been allowed to tell Libby about? It was possible, but unlikely. Libby had been sent here to shadow Antonia, to learn from her. As far as she'd been led to believe, they had the same clearance. There was no reason for Libby not to know Antonia's schedule.

Libby shook her head, and put each drive in a separate place in her purse, making sure she knew which one was which. She tucked the device reader back into the shopping bag, beneath the folds of tissue paper that covered some new items from the high-end store, just as the taxi pulled up at her destination.

Whatever weirdness was going on with Antonia, the bottom line was that Libby had a job to do.

She'd worry about the rest of it later.

ANTONIA SLIPPED INTO THE BLACK SKIRT THAT SKIMMED just below her knees and the plain white button-down shirt, pairing the outfit with low-heeled black pumps. Added a wig:

a short black bob. About as unassuming an outfit she could put together, rendering herself as invisible as she could manage.

She was sweating. Moving too quickly in this stifling, monk's cell excuse for an apartment. Speed was of the essence, but not so much that she'd make a mistake. She took another long, slow breath in, out, calming herself.

She considered calling their boss, claiming Libby had gone rogue or some other excuse that would get Libby's fake passport blocked so she couldn't enter the party. But there was no telling how long that would take, and it would put the spotlight on Antonia, too.

She couldn't risk that.

She had to do this herself.

She grabbed one of her few extravagances: a breathtakingly expensive tote bag, buttery-soft black Italian leather with gold buckles. She stashed in it the passports and money, and a few other essentials she'd need over the next few days.

She'd planned to just leave, but now she had to get the thumb drive back first.

When the apartment door stuck, she didn't bother to yank it all the way shut, much less lock it, before she headed down the worn wooden staircase. Let someone steal everything. It wasn't her problem anymore. She wouldn't be coming back.

And depending on how things went down, Libby might not, either.

THE COCKTAIL PARTY WAS BEING HELD AT CASA MARTELLI, a fifteenth-century house that had been turned into a museum, still preserved in its original state to show how a wealthy Medici-era family would have lived. Libby had been on the guided tour already; she'd taken advantage of being stationed in Florence by hitting all the sites.

She handed her ID to the black-suited security guard at the door. He scanned it, glanced at the information that came up on his tablet.

"Welcome, Signora Parker," he said in accented English as he handed her passport back.

"Grazie," she responded. "Is there a place I can safely put this?" She held up the shopping bag.

He directed her to a small room set up as a coat check, where a bored attendant—nobody had coats to check on this still-warm evening—took her bag, gave her a numbered ticket, and set the bag next to a short line of leather briefcases, no doubt from diplomats stopping at the party on their way home from work.

She glanced at the slim gold watch on her wrist. She was actually a few minutes early. She had time to order a glass of Pellegrino fizzy water from the bar and fill a tiny plate with a few delicacies: prosciutto-wrapped melon; carefully stacked slices of red tomatoes, fresh white mozzarella and green basil leaves; glistening black caviar on toast points topped with a tiny dollop of cream.

One of the rules was, eat when you can safely do so. You never know where your next meal will be coming from, or what it might contain.

Libby made her way through the room of gold wallpaper, the blue-painted room covered in paintings and a very prominent crucifix, and finally to the one of the rooms with its walls covered with frescoes.

The Winter Garden Room had supposedly been painted to make up for the fact that the house had no outdoor garden space. It was breathtaking. Vines trailed up columns and across the vaulted ceiling. Vine-covered arches opened onto scenes of the city, or of fountains with the setting sun glowing in the distance.

Libby eased her way between partygoers to reach a wall near one corner. Between two painted, vine-spiraled columns and beneath an actual real window, two painted cats played at the edge of a fountain.

She finished her hors d'oeuvres, passed the plate to a red-vested waiter, and sipped her Pellegrino.

A moment later, a man stepped up next to her.

As expected, he wore a pink pocket square with slate-grey dots in his grey suit jacket.

She made a miniscule gesture with her glass. "I believe cats to be spirits come to earth."

"A cat, I am sure, could walk on a cloud without coming through," he said, finishing the Jules Verne quote and thus confirming himself as her contact.

He was a tall black man, handsome despite the acne scars pitting his cheeks. Or perhaps because of; they gave his face character.

They both spoke Italian, but his had the slightest of French accents beneath.

"You're not who I expected," he said. His expression didn't change, but she heard the thread of suspicion in his voice.

Shit. Antonia should have let her handler know Libby would be making the exchange, allowing the information to pass through the appropriate channels.

Maybe there hadn't been time.

Then again, the second flash drive put Antonia under suspicion in a major way.

Libby had to decide what to do, and fast.

Antonia had the taxi driver drop her off a block and a half away from Casa Martelli. She would have done that in any instance, to disguise her true destination and to give her time to see if she'd been followed. But Casa Martelli was sandwiched in between shops, the entire block of buildings snugging up against each other as if expecting a siege. The only way to the back door was through narrow alleys twisting between those buildings, accessible one street over.

The air cooled a few degrees in the high-walled alleys where the slanted rays of the sun didn't reach. Pigeons cooed in the recesses in the bricks high above as the street noise faded the deeper she went.

Antonia knocked at the back door of Casa Martelli. She had to wait several minutes before someone answered, a harried-looking man who opened the door with an exasperated "What?" in Italian.

Well, dammit. She'd gotten the white button-down and black skirt right, but the waitstaff uniforms for this function apparently also included red vests.

If you were dressed similarly enough, were pretty (or handsome) without being overly so, and had a tray of drinks or delectable-looking morsels, nobody noticed you weren't in the exact uniform of the rest of the waitstaff.

Now, she could either stay with her initial plan of sweet-talking her way in, claiming to be a member of the staff who had gotten lost (and forgotten her vest), or she could go with Plan B.

She'd stick out like a sore thumb without the vest. Plan B it was.

She spoke softly, indicating her throat as if to imply she had laryngitis, and used a mix of broken Italian and English.

The waiter leaned close to hear her.

She jammed the syringe into his neck.

His eyes widened and he gave a short bark of surprise, but

thankfully nobody heard. The drug didn't knock him out immediately, but made him both woozy and pliable as it entered his bloodstream. Antonia was able to support him, stumbling, around the corner of the alley, where he finally collapsed. Good. Another member of the waitstaff stepping outside for a cigarette wouldn't see him.

He wouldn't come to until she was well gone, and he'd have a spot of amnesia covering a few hours before his attack.

It took a few moments to roll him this way and that so she could strip the vest off him. It was far too big for her, but she grabbed a few safety pins from her tote and nipped in the seams, which helped.

She pulled a plastic trash bag from her tote and stuffed the tote into it, setting the bag in the small pile of trash already by the back door. She'd do what she needed to do and be back before anyone cleared away the garbage.

Then she slipped inside, grabbed a tray of bacon-wrapped figs, and popped one in her mouth. The bacon had been soaked in maple syrup, and the taste was incredible.

Tray in hand, she entered the cocktail party.

LIBBY TAPPED THE GOLD-AND-PEARL PIN AT HER SHOULDER, activating the sound cancelling that would pick the ambient music—a string quartet in the next room—rather than their conversation.

"I think my partner has been compromised," she said to her contact. "She sent me here in her place. Check the information on the drive carefully. She tried to replace it, but I found what I believe is the original, which I'm giving to you."

"Why don't you give me both?" he asked.

Fair question. "I need proof about what she's done."

He nodded slowly, and reached into his pocket, presumably to retrieve the drive he'd exchange for hers.

She'd turned from the frescoed wall once he'd arrived, keeping a casual eye on the room. She saw Antonia, dressed as waitstaff in an ill-fitting red vest, a black wig not disguise enough. She froze.

"She's here," she murmured. "I have to go. We'll reschedule the drop. I'm sorry."

He was already scanning the crowd, but Libby was gone, ducking left and then right through the partygoers, losing herself in the small crowd. It wasn't easy at her height, but most people had imbibed at least one drink, and she'd learned how to hunch, to make herself less obvious.

Her heart pounded in her throat. Antonia must have discovered the missing thumb drive faster than Libby had expected.

If Antonia wanted that drive, she'd stop at nothing to get it. Libby was sure of that. Antonia might be a casual slob, might take her duties lightly, but she had an undercurrent of steeliness that she'd tried to hide from Libby.

Unbeknownst to Antonia, she'd failed at that.

Libby threw her ticket at the coat check attendant and forced herself not to grab her own bag, but let the attendant hand it to her. She had to not be too obvious, too memorable. That meant people would pay attention. Remember her.

She ducked into the ladies room, locked the door, and yanked things out of her shopping bag.

A few moments later, she exited the back door—the waitstaff were too busy to notice her, even as unassuming as she was.

Her shapeless black dress was padded so she looked heavier, and she hunched her shoulders. She'd changed her shoes to black, soft-soled laceups, one of which had a pebble in it to throw her gait off, make her limp slightly. Half of her hair was shoved under a big straw hat that obscured her face; the other half straggled down, giving the impression that her hair was thinner than it was.

The rest of her belongings, including the high-end shopping bag, were stuff in a generic woven-string market bag.

All of it told the casual eye: I'm old. I'm nobody. I'm an average, unassuming Italian matriarch headed home to make dinner.

It was only a ten-minute walk to the Arno River, but she took a good forty minutes, wandering down alleys and side streets, alert to any sign of a tail.

LIBBY WAS GOOD—ANTONIA WOULD GIVE HER THAT MUCH. It didn't surprise Antonia; Libby surely would have taken her training seriously, focused on doing everything right.

Unfortunately for Libby, Antonia had put a tracking software on her phone ages ago. If Libby ever found it, Antonia would have said it was a test to see how fast Libby found it. She hadn't thus far.

So as soon as Antonia figured out where Libby was going, she abandoned trying to track her through the streets and doubled back.

She knew how to get there first.

Libby was stepping onto Ponte Vecchio, one of the most famous bridges in the world.

Dating back to the Middle Ages, the stone bridge over the Arno River was lined with shops along each side. Originally butcher shops, they now housed primarily jewelry shops catering to the tourists.

Tourists who were still crowding the bridge on this balmy summer evening, taking advantage of the later shopping hours. Now that the sun had set, the air had cooled, soft on Antonia's face.

Libby would have to fight her way through that throng... but there was another way across the Ponte Vecchio.

In the sixteenth century, Cosimo de Medici had ordered built an enclosed corridor along the top of the shops to ease his passage between his palace and the town hall. About ten years ago, the Vasari Corridor had been opened for public tours. Then, last year, it had been closed again for maintenance.

Antonia knew where the entrance was on this side of the river.

Either Libby intended to lose herself in the crowd—in which case Antonia would be waiting for her on the other side—or Libby knew of another entrance to the corridor—in which case Antonia would meet her inside.

And if Libby doubled back, the tracking software would let Antonia know. She could be at either end before Libby.

Then she could get the damn thumb drive back, hopefully the drive from their contact as well, and be on her way to her money and freedom.

She wasn't going to let by-the-rules Libby ruin everything for her.

LIBBY CUT HER WAY THROUGH THE CROWD, OCCASIONALLY murmuring, "Scusami. Scusami, grazie." People paid her little mind, barely glanced at her. Her hip hurt, thanks to the pebble that made her limp. She was dearly looking forward to fixing that problem.

It was no doubt the least of her problems.

But she was close to her goal, and she hadn't spotted a tail. She hunched a little shorter, continuing to make her height less conspicuous and give the impression of age. Her soft-soled shoes made no sound on the stone bridge, not that footsteps would be audible above the sounds of chattering tourists.

About a quarter of the way down, she ducked into a shop between the glass cases that bordered the door. She nodded at the shop clerk, and asked, in Italian, for Mondavian gold.

Something that didn't exist.

The man nodded in recognition and drew her to the back of the shop as if to show her what she sought. Once the shop was empty, she slipped through the door into the back storage area.

Then it was a simple matter of sliding a shelving unit sideways, unlocking the door behind it, sliding the shelf back after she'd entered the tiny room, and squeezing into a corner so she could swing the door back shut and lock it again.

She'd paid the shopkeepers handsomely for this, after poring over schematics of the Ponte Vecchio and the Vasari Corridor—private schematics she'd also paid handsomely for the privilege of viewing.

The room she was now in was little more than a wide square chimney with ancient iron hand- and footholds affixed into the stone, leading up. The only light was from a tiny bit that bled around the door from the shop's storage room, but Libby had done this once with a flashlight in her teeth, and didn't need more practice than that.

She climbed the ladder, counting the rungs to know when she'd reached the top. Then, she unlocked the door there and entered a storage closet, and from there stepped into the Vasari Corridor.

The floor was brick-red tiles in a herringbone pattern; the walls were pale cream. No paintings hung on the walls now, as they did when the passageway was open for tours. The evenly spaced windows high on the outer wall didn't provide light now at night, but a series of pale emergency lights along the wall near the floor, each about a foot long with a molded opaque white cover, gave a little illumination.

Just enough to see the hulking outlines of the scaffolding, the piles of materials, the locked toolboxes.

Antonia had impressed upon her the importance of stashing a go-bag somewhere in the city, in case she had to leave quickly but couldn't get back to the apartment. The train station lockers made sense, because it made it easy to leave by public transportation. Antonia probably had a bag stashed there, too.

Libby seriously doubted Antonia knew she had this one.

She popped open the front casing one of the small modern light fixtures near the floor and used the folds of her skirt to protect her fingers as she removed the hot bulb. Then she carefully unscrewed the fixture, and reached behind to find the small canvas bag she'd left there.

Passport, money, a burner phone. The bare essentials for an escape, in case she was compromised and in danger, and the American Embassy wasn't an option.

She shoved it into her string bag, then removed her shoe and shook out the offending pebble. She didn't bother to replace the light. So what if someone came across it tomorrow? She'd be long gone.

She leaned against the wall. She'd wait a bit, just to make sure no one had followed her onto the Ponte Vecchio below.

Then she heard a noise down the corridor. A metallic hum, as if someone had brushed against scaffolding, then stopped the vibration with their hand on the piping.

Not breathing, Libby slowly, silently reached for her gun, and hid it in the folds of her skirt.

Antonia—or someone—had found her after all.

Antonia crept forward, barefoot, her shoes in her tote. The bare, enclosed corridor would amplify footsteps. She'd barely brushed against the scaffolding, and caught it a moment after it hummed, but she still cursed herself, cursed her eyes that hadn't fully adjusted to the dim emergency lights.

Couldn't be helped now.

She was rushing too much. Picking the lock without being seen had taken longer than she'd expected. The noises she'd heard up ahead must be Libby.

She was so over this. Over Florence, over Libby, over the job.

That was no reason to get sloppy, though.

So she changed her tactic and walked up to Libby as if she owned the damn place.

"What are you doing hiding in here, Libby?" she asked. "This isn't part of the drop."

Libby was on her feet, standing next to the net shopping bag she'd been carrying. Her hand was half-hidden in the folds of her skirt. Probably concealing her gun.

She wouldn't shoot unless she had to, though. Libby's training was solid, and she followed rules. Antonia could use that to her advantage, if it came to it.

"I ended up with two thumb drives," Libby said. "That was weird, so I knew something was up. I thought it would be safer to lie low and monitor the situation."

Antonia mentally rolled her eyes. "You panicked. And your disguise wasn't nearly good enough: I picked you out right away."

"So why'd it take you so long to get to me?" Libby asked.

"*I* was monitoring *you*," Antonia said. "This was a test."

Libby shook her head. "If this was a test, then call HQ and have them confirm it."

Well, it had been worth a try.

"Just give me the thumb drive, Libby."

"I don't have it," Libby said. "I made the exchange."

"Then give me the drive you received."

"I don't have it on me."

"Then take me to it," Antonia said. "Just give me one of the drives—one of the real drives—and I'll be out of your hair."

"You haven't been following me around Florence just to get the drive and let me go," Libby said.

"Okay, then," Antonia said amiably, because she'd long guessed it was going to come to this. "Then I'll shoot you and take the drive."

She saw Libby's hand move in the folds of her skirt.

Two painfully loud reports, almost simultaneous, slammed through the corridor.

LIBBY'S EARS RANG, ACHING FROM THE GUNSHOT. BUT SHE was alive, somehow. She'd brought her gun out, but Antonia had been faster....

Now, as Antonia spun and crumpled to the ground, crimson blossoming on the front of her white button-down blouse, Libby stared in shock at the tall black man who'd come up behind Antonia. Her contact from the cocktail party.

"How did you...?" She automatically spoke in Italian.

He shrugged as he stepped forward, sliding his gun under his jacket. "When I saw your partner leave after you, I followed her. She didn't expect a tail, so she never noticed. Sloppy."

Libby's cheek stung. She touched it, and in the dim light saw plaster dust and a smear of blood. Antonia's shot had just missed Libby's head, ricocheting off the plaster wall. Some of the plaster must have grazed her.

"But why?" Libby asked the man, her mind spinning through possible scenarios. Her heart was slowing to normal, thanks to her training.

"You said she might be compromised, and I was concerned for your safety. I don't leave fellow agents behind."

Libby knelt beside Antonia's body. Antonia's gun had fallen next to her hand, half under her lifeless form. She leaned closer, peering at her. "That's odd," she said.

"What?" the other agent asked, squatting down on the other side of the body.

Libby shot him in the head with Antonia's gun.

"I'm sorry," she said, only half-meaning it. His damn gallantry had ruined everything. He'd expect her to come with him, sort things out together, be her backup when she gave her report—and she didn't have time for any of that. Her cover was blown here, and he was the only witness. She had to get away before anyone else in the American agency came looking for her or Antonia.

Libby eased the gun, which she'd held in the fabric of her skirt to avoid leaving prints, into Antonia's hand. Let them sort out who'd killed who, the hows and the whys of it.

As for Antonia... Libby sniffed as she checked the woman's pockets for anything useful—or incriminating. Antonia wasn't much better than a child playing at spycraft. She'd fallen so easily for Libby's ruses: the pretense of following rules, the neatness, the good humor.

Of course, they all had. She'd found it amusing to go through all the training a second time in a new country, passing herself off as an American, never quite doing things perfectly so she didn't stand out, didn't look suspicious. Learning a few secrets along the way.

Her assignment had been to stay deeply imbedded in the American system, but this incident changed things.

It was time to go home.

Elizaveta Papanova was going home, out of the sticky humidity and back to the crisp, chill air of her beloved Russia....

At least until her next assignment.

BOTHERING WITH THE DETAILS

Lydia Menchin finished her crossword puzzle in record time, which would have been a success except she'd been trying to stretch the time out. Now her surroundings flowed back into her consciousness: the slightly bitter scent of coffee, the light jazz on the sound system occasionally overcome by the harsh buzz of the coffee grinder, the hard wooden chair that made her bones ache.

She was pretty sure Starbucks had uncomfortable chairs so customers wouldn't sit there all day. That and the air conditioning that was always a little too cold (especially on days like today, when the fog crept in and shrouded San Jose in gloom). They were effective ploys.

She'd never been without a job before, and the passing minutes wore on her like water dripping on a rock.

She'd worked as an editor all her life, usually in places where the hustle and bustle of the office flowed around her. Newspapers were the worst—people always on the phone, and first typewriters, then keyboards clacking away.

Dayken Tech, her last employer, had been the best in that sense—everybody staring silently at their monitors, meetings held behind closed conference room doors—but by the time she'd started working there, she'd become inured to background noise and distractions.

Lydia believed she could find a single typo in a 500-page document in the middle of a war zone with missiles screaming by.

She'd tuned out Starbuck's for a little while now, except for absentmindedly slipping on her favorite cardigan, a soft sage-green wool, between finishing Across and starting Down.

Lydia could've gone home, but she'd recently allowed her granddaughter, Brittani, to move in with her while Brittani attended Stanford, and she wanted to give the girl some space to study. Unlike Lydia, Brittani seemed to need quiet to concentrate, and the apartment wasn't that large. Comfortable enough for one, less so for two independent adults.

The crossword done and the rest of the newspaper read, Lydia turned her attention to her iPad and checked Craigslist for editing jobs. There were ads for writers of various types (but she had no interest in that, happy to leave the writing to the writers. Her job was to make their writing shine.), a fair number of obvious scams, and one or two positions involving blogging and SEO and on-page optimization and so forth.

All of the publishers and newspapers and magazines and even major websites in the Bay Area had her résumé, but no one wanted to hire a woman near retirement age when they could get some wet-behind-the-ears thing at half the price.

Half the knowledge and experience, too, but everybody thought the job was easy. Find a few typos. Know the difference between "lie" and "lay."

Lydia snorted. Child's play.

She was the best copyeditor she knew, and she was probably one of the best copyeditors in the country. She might phrase it more humbly to a prospective employer, but she would also give examples of her expertise.

Her son had once gotten her a bumper sticker that said "CMOS 6.18"—referring to the rule of the glorious Oxford comma. Because she thought stickers and vanity plates were tacky, she'd stuck it on on her fridge with a magnet that said "The past, the present, and the future walked into a bar. It was tense."

The Chicago Manual of Style: that was her bible, the holy book of her religion, and she'd read it more times than the Pope had read the Christian Bible. (CMOS 14.254 discussed how to properly cite different versions of the Bible.)

Problem was, Dayken Tech—and, she was pretty sure, anywhere else she'd sent her résumé—assumed she couldn't keep up with the technology. When Dayken had gone from a paper-based shareholder newsletter to an electronic one, and added a blog, well, that's when they'd let Lydia go.

As if she hadn't already memorized Considerations for Web-Based Publications, CMOS 1.111–1.117. She already knew enough to edit Dayken's manuals. And just because she was older didn't mean she didn't know basic technology. She'd been an early adopter of the word processor, one of the first to encourage authors to send electronic files so she could use Track Changes. She was familiar with web design as it related to proofreading. She wasn't some doddering grandma who couldn't figure out how to program the DVR.

Dayken was still an up-and-coming company, though, and Lydia continued to invest in them, even after she'd left. She sipped her cooling Earl Grey (another victim of the air conditioning) and called up the company blog on her iPad.

It was true that she didn't understand software coding at all, but she'd worked there long enough to understand what it took to roll out a new product, so she followed the tech news.

The person editing the copy on the Dayken Tech blog,

though...yeesh. Oh, there were no outright spelling errors or egregious punctuation mistakes, and the format was clean enough (you didn't have control over everything when it came to online formatting), but there was always something.

Multiple somethings.

They were mistakes the average reader would never notice...but Lydia, of course, did.

That subhead had inconsistent capitalization from all the others at the same level (CMOS 2.56, Editing subheads). There was irregular use of the CFO's middle initial (8.3, Personal names—additional resources). And so on.

It was a nightmare. (A literal nightmare—Lydia had woken up just two nights ago from a horrible dream about chasing someone down to stop them before they hit "Send" on the stockholder's newsletter...because the company name was spelled wrong.)

And she knew who was responsible. She wasn't supposed to know who they hired to replace her, but she'd been in Human Resources for her exit interview and seen the résumé on the desk, the one from someone applying for the position of Media Relations Assistant. Lydia's job.

It had been on a pile marked New Hirees. She'd been replaced before she'd even left the building.

Lydia would never forget the woman's name: Danielle Gilbert.

Pressing her lips together, Lydia recorded the mistakes in a notebook, along with the date and the CMOS references. Eventually she'd have enough to send to Francis, the head of Media Relations.

***

Over the weeks, Lydia amassed a disheartening and,

frankly, embarrassing (for Dayken Tech) number of errors on their blog.

The most annoying thing was, only a few of the mistakes were consistent. The rest were all over the map. One week, 5.9 (Mass noun followed by a prepositional phrase), was used correctly; the next week, it wasn't. Sometimes the "s" in a plural italicized word was italicized itself (correctly), and sometimes it wasn't (clearly covered in 7.11—sigh). Further vs. farther. Abbreviations with and without periods.

Lydia's head hurt.

A bit of sun today, and even though the Bay Area didn't have proper seasons, you could call this Indian summer, a brief spate of warmer weather before autumn really took hold, so she had the windows open in her small apartment.

The fresh air made the place feel less cramped. It was the third story of a Victorian, with two bedrooms and one bathroom. The natural, dark wood hadn't been painted, the original white-and-black hexagonal tile still graced the bathroom floor, none of the floors were exactly straight, and Lydia loved the place. She'd moved here almost fifteen years ago after the last of her kids had left the nest and her husband soon followed, because apparently the only thing they'd had in common in the end was the kids. It had been amicable enough, and they caught up at weddings and birthday parties and the like.

Her office had been in the second bedroom, but when Brittani moved in, Lydia had moved her desk into a closet and downsized as best she could. She was glad to give her granddaughter a place to stay, and Brittani did chip in for rent and utilities, and because she liked to cook, she made dinner a couple of nights a week, if her studies weren't too crazy.

Dinner, and chocolate-chip cookies. Brittani was really good at those, and the apartment was currently filled with the tantalizing aroma from the batch Brittani had made before classes today.

Lydia had just returned from a disastrous job interview. She knew with her hair tastefully dyed and her trim figure (she did senior aerobics three times a week and swam laps on Saturdays), she looked a decade younger than her real age. But the barely-out-of-college-aged man who interviewed her clearly didn't think editing was all that important, and offered her what amounted to a secretarial typing job for a third of the salary she'd commanded earlier.

Pointing out the errors in their want ad had not helped the process one bit.

Between her investments and Brittani's contributions, Lydia was doing fine. She didn't *need* another job, really. She was just *bored*, and was tired of reading things with subpar editing. At least when she was working, she felt she was helping stem the tide of sloppiness in some small way.

By the time Brittani came home from class, Lydia was in her big, comfy, burgundy leather club chair, nursing a martini, her editing notes from the Dayken Tech website lined up on the matching ottoman.

Brittani was tall and lanky, with auburn hair in a cute pixie cut and a semicolon tattoo on the inside of her left ring finger. Lydia knew what the tattoo meant, and approved of the symbolic reminder that depression lied.

"Is this a new kind of Sudoku? I thought you didn't like playing with numbers, Nonna," Brittani said, looking at the pages of notes.

"No, I still leave that to people like you," Lydia said. "These are sections of *The Chicago Manual of Style*."

But Brittani had dropped her backpack and come around to stand next to the chair and see the pages right side up.

"Really?" she said. "Because some of these—" she pointed

to a few different lines "—look like a simple substitution cypher."

"What do you mean?"

"A substitution cypher is where you substitute something else for letters. The simplest one is replacing the letters of the alphabet with numbers: A is 1, B is 2, and so on." Brittani pointed again. "So these all end with the same letters: DAYKENCOM."

"How can you read that so fast?" Lydia asked. She had barely started counting on her fingers.

Brittani laughed. "I'm a nerd, Nonna. Remember my friend Charlotte? In fifth grade, all we did was send coded messages to each other. Words are your thing—numbers are mine."

Which was why Brittani was studying something computer engineering related that Lydia didn't quite understand (but enough to copyedit Brittani's papers).

"So what does the rest of it say?" she asked. She explained that the numbers came from the CMOS sections of errors she'd found on the Dayken Tech blog. "I used to work there," she added, "and dayken dot com was the email domain."

"That makes sense," Brittani said. "This one says KUJONESDAYKENCOM."

"Kumar Jones," Lydia said. "He's the head of research."

Brittani read off more names, and Lydia recognized most of them as people who worked in research and development at the company, or other high executives.

"What about the rest of it?" she asked.

Brittani shook her head. "No obvious name or word patterns. Mostly random numbers and letters. And different ones attached to the same email addresses on each page."

"Each page is the list of mistakes on one weekly blog or the investor newsletter," Lydia said slowly, thinking. The same email addresses didn't show up every week, but they did repeat, and when they did, they had different random letters and numbers attached to them. What changed weekly...?

Oh.

"Passwords," she said. "Could they be passwords? Dayken had pretty strict access restrictions, and they used rolling passwords that changed at least once a week."

Brittani grabbed Lydia's martini and took a hefty swallow. Lydia didn't mind. She'd made a pitcher—and they both needed it now.

"So someone is sending coded messages to tell someone else what the newest passwords are," Brittani said. "Does Dayken have a VPN?"

"In English?" Lydia requested.

"Sorry. Virtual private network. It allows employees to access the company computer system from anywhere."

Lydia had worked at home a few times when she had a cold and didn't want to infect her co-workers. "Yes."

"Then with this information and the VPN, anyone could access the company network," Brittani said, nodding slowly.

Lydia had to revise her opinion of Danielle Gilbert, who'd taken her job. Danielle wasn't a bad copyeditor after all—she knew CMOS almost as well as Lydia did—and she was a corporate spy.

WHEN LYDIA HAD WORKED AT DAYKEN, SHE'D BECOME good friends with Sandy Kirchner, assistant to the CEO, Miles Grunberg. Sandy was a few years older than Lydia, and had worked for Miles's father at his company. Miles had inherited her when he started his own tech start-up, and by all accounts found her indispensable. She was, apparently, never allowed to retire.

Dayken's campus was laid out with a network of wide,

white cement walking paths that meandered through carefully placed trees and landscaping. At break times, there were always people jogging or walking. Lydia and Sandy had bonded during their daily brisk jaunt at lunchtime.

The day after Lydia and Brittani had found the pattern, Lydia met up with Sandy for a walk—it was another sunny, cool day—and it took only a few minutes before Sandy offered to set up a meeting between Lydia and Miles.

"This is huge," Sandy breathed. "Like, *they should make a movie out of this* huge."

"Okay, but only if Helen Mirren plays me," Lydia said.

"Dammit," Sandy said. "I wanted Helen Mirren."

"You can have Judi Dench," Lydia offered.

Sandy was good with that.

⁂

MILES AGREED TO SEE LYDIA THAT EVENING. THEY WERE joined by Steve Mignardi—Lydia's old boss, the head of Media Relations, and Danielle's current boss.

Even at the time, Lydia had been pretty sure Steve had been pressured by the money people to cut costs, and given her salary, she'd been an obvious candidate for the layoff (if stupid from a quality control angle). So she didn't blame him —much.

She still let him squirm a little as he said it was good to see her and asked how she was doing.

Miles Grunburg was about as old as Lydia's oldest son. Short and compact, he looked like someone who ran every day. His blond hair was in an easy-care buzz cut, and he always wore blue and yellow company polo shirts and chinos.

Steve, on the other hand, was tall and skinny, with thick, unruly black hair, dark eyes, and an Italian nose.

Lydia had never been in Miles's office before. Floor-to-ceiling windows looked out over the network of paths and trees and clumps of flowers, but his desk faced the other way, and she got the sense he wasn't much for gazing at nature. His U-shaped cherrywood desk was cluttered with papers, circuit boards (and other bits she couldn't identify), three wide flat screen monitors. A recycling bin was heaped with Mt Dew cans.

In one corner was a small, casual conference area with a coffee table that matched the desk, and a sofa and several easy chairs covered with blue-and-yellow fabric patterned with the Dayken logo. There was a glass bowl of those cutie oranges on the table. When they all sat, Steve grabbed one and started to peel it, but Miles gave him a look, and Steve set it back down.

Lydia pulled the notebook pages and her iPad out of her large handbag, and set the iPad on the table. Pushing the bowl aside, she spread out the pages, then pulled up the Dayken blog.

And she explained everything.

It took a little while, because Miles had never heard of CMOS—but he *had* heard of corporate espionage, and Dayken *was* rolling out a new product soon that was secret enough to have a code name, which was Flowerpot. Lydia thought that was sort of sweet.

"Tell me about Danielle," Miles said to Steve, with a *you hired her* squint in his blue eyes.

Steve shrugged helplessly. "I thought she was doing a good job," he said. He glanced at Lydia. "Guess I was wrong."

Miles stood. "Ms. Menchin," he said, "thank you for bringing this to our attention."

Lydia didn't get up. "What are you going to do?"

Miles blinked, apparently so taken aback by Lydia not just leaving that he wasn't sure what to do for a moment. "What do you mean?" he asked finally.

"I mean," Lydia said, "that you need more proof, don't you? Couldn't Danielle argue that someone else was doing this? She and I aren't the only people in the world who know how to copyedit."

Miles sat back down. Steve said, "How can we prove it's her?"

"I've thought of that, too," Lydia said, allowing herself a grim smile.

THE NEXT BLOG WAS SCHEDULED TO BE POSTED TUESDAY AT midnight—Wednesday, really (CMOS 9.39). The plan was this:

Steve would give the blog to Danielle to edit on Tuesday afternoon as usual. But he'd tell her to save it as a draft, not set it to go live at midnight, because he was waiting on some last-minute information. If it came in after she'd gone home, she could still make the update remotely and schedule the publication. This happened frequently enough that it shouldn't raise a red flag for her.

Instead, however, he'd have Lydia correct any mistakes in Danielle's edit, thus removing the coded message.

Steve would then text Danielle to say not to worry, the new info didn't arrive after all, so he set the post to go live himself—after he fixed a few typos.

Lydia, Steve, and Miles were in Miles's when Steve sent the text. Then they waited.

The IT department had already found evidence on Danielle's computer that proved she'd gained access to the password system.

When Danielle logged in remotely, and they watched her re-edit the things Lydia had corrected, then re-published the post, she pounded the final nail into her own coffin.

Plus Lydia had changed other things Danielle hadn't even noticed, so whatever her partner in crime decoded, it wouldn't be correct.

"I'd like to see Danielle's face tomorrow when she comes in and gets arrested," Lydia said.

"I don't think that would be the best idea," Miles said. "But we *would* like you to come in tomorrow."

"Oh?" she asked, although she guessed what was coming.

Steve cleared his throat. "We'd like to offer you your job back. Two percent raise, same benefits."

Lydia pondered. "An extra week's vacation and more stock options," she countered.

"That can be arranged," Miles said. "I'll have HR draw up the contract in the morning."

Lydia smiled. *Finally*, someone recognized what her talents were really worth.

WHY DON'T YOU MAKE GINGERBREAD?

My cookie boutique, Rebecca's Cookie Confections, is popular all year, but unsurprisingly, orders increase exponentially during the holidays.

I make sugar cookies sprinkled with festively colored sugars, and peppermint meltaways and peanut butter thumbprints. Pistachio-cranberry rugelach, Italian Christmas cookies, Norwegian wreaths, Swedish snowballs, and more

And every year, I get the same question, over and over, in some format:

Why don't you make gingerbread?

Because people talk, and would likely compare answers over a glass of Chard while they bitch about the lack of gingerbread available from my shop, I give the same general answer:

I've never quite gotten the hang of gingerbread. Or, *I haven't created the perfect recipe for gingerbread.*

This would be a lie.

If I told the truth, I'd be out of business faster than I could sift a cup of flour. And I can do that mighty fast.

MRS. SHIRLEY GILMORE WASN'T EXACTLY ONE OF THOSE sweet little old ladies of Farrows County. Her hair was dyed bright red and teased for height, allowing glimpses of her pink scalp. Her green eyes were bright and sharp, but not unkind, behind bifocals, and she was sinewy-thin like some women get when they age.

She volunteered at the library for as long as anyone could remember, including organizing the annual book sale so well that nobody wanted to volunteer for the position.

No pets, no Mr. Gilmore in anyone's memory (the consensus was that she'd moved to our neighborhood after being widowed), just a sturdy Cadillac that kept on ticking and a well-tended yard with a few beds of flowers and herbs, and a lawn the teenage boys looking for extra cash mowed in the summer and a driveway they shoveled in the winter.

And, most importantly, the best gingerbread anyone had ever tasted, which she generously shared at the holidays with everyone who'd crossed her path that year.

Neighbors. The aforementioned teenage boys. Anyone who'd worked on the library book sale as well the library staff. Her doctor's office. Her hairdresser. The mechanic that kept that old Caddy running. Friends from the senior center where she took Yoga for the Mature classes and attended biweekly dances where the women outnumbered the men two to one (and, of course, the yoga instructor and the dance coordinator). Police stations and fire stations and homeless shelters and nursery schools, oh my.

She started baking right after Thanksgiving, and kept on going until Christmas, with deliveries continuing until New Year's Eve. She did it all by herself, too.

Until I came along, that is.

I was about ten years old when my father chose his secretary over us and my mother went back to work full-time as an attorney., which brought up the need for me to be watched over after school, and on the occasional weekends when her job demanded it.

Our house was on the end of the street, and Mrs. Gilmore lived three doors down and across the street. The houses on our side had long, sloping lawns that lead to a wide river, and the houses on the other side had smaller lawns that ended against a tangle of trees

All the houses had huge front and back yards, and generous space between them, marooning us in a sea of green in the summer and white in the winter like distant islands.

My mother must have been friends with Mrs. Gilmore, because suddenly I found myself deposited at Mrs. Gilmore's home with the explanation that she would be watching over me.

The arrangement was more than fine for me. I was a bookish girl, preferring fiction to reality, and Mrs. Gilmore's house was a glittering dragon's hoard of books.

Her house was built in the late sixties or early seventies, a one-story with high ceilings and a wide hallway along which all the rooms grew. Kitchen, dining room, living room, bedrooms. The first weekend I spent there, for dinner Mrs. Gilmore made French bread pizzas that I burned the roof of my mouth on, and then she ushered me to a bedroom that had a bed snugged up between floor-to-ceiling bookcases, all made of dark wood.

I plucked something off the shelves, inhaling the vanilla scent of older books, and read late into the night, and then late into the morning, stumbling out at a time that would have horrified my mother. Mrs. Gilmore gave me sandwiches and nudged me back to the living room, which was ringed by more bookcases.

I can't say we bonded, Mrs. Gilmore and I, that weekend.

Looking back, I can see she didn't know quite what to do with me, and was probably relieved when she discovered she didn't have to monitor me.

So I came to Mrs. Gilmore's after school and did whatever homework I hadn't finished in study hall, then read until my mother came home.

Until Thanksgiving, and the beginning of the annual gingerbread baking extravaganza.

In truth, the first year I tucked into one corner of the nubbly turquoise sofa in the living room and lost myself in another book—except that the pungent scents of ginger and sugar kept invading my senses, the aroma wafting into my consciousness as it did in Saturday morning cartoons, a visible curling mist targeting my nostrils.

The following year, however, I put down whatever I was reading and wandered to the entrance of the kitchen. Mrs. Gilmore was rolling out dough and humming tunelessly.

"Can I help?"

She jumped and turned, her hands pressing into the avocado-green counter.

"I'm sorry I startled you," I said, because I was raised to be polite. "I just wondered if I could help. I'd love to learn how to bake."

My mother was too busy to teach me to cook, although I'd learned a few basic dishes out of self-preservation. I might have been a daydreaming bookworm, but something about baking tugged at me. Mrs. Gilmore presented an opportunity.

Her lips pursed, highlighting the lines around her mouth into which her lipstick had bled. Sweat beaded her upper lip, and her unnaturally red updo tendriled around her face in the heat of the kitchen. She pondered my query, her sharp green eyes a spotlight that I couldn't squirm away from.

Then she glanced around the kitchen.

Along with the generous counters, the appliances were

also avocado green. The floor tiles were a pattern that included that particular hue. The sink, your basic stainless-steel twofer, was on a half wall separating the kitchen from an eating area, the dishwasher beside the sink. Above the counters and sink, dark-stained cabinets with plain pewter-colored handles

And on all the counters as well as on the black, round kitchen table were the implements of her project: flour and spices, eggs, bowls, trays, and a rolling pin crafted out of pale marble shot through with gray.

The humidity from the heat of the double ovens built into the wall was thick with ginger and vanilla and cinnamon. Steam bathed the windows, separating us from the outside world.

I didn't know the weight of the question I'd asked.

Mrs. Gilmore was nice to me, in a distant way, and she let me read anything I wanted whether it was "appropriate" or not, and I wanted to learn how to bake. To me, it was simple enough.

Had someone grabbed my arm and said, "No, Rebecca, don't go down that road," I'm not sure I would have listened to them. I loved my mother, and I didn't think she'd abandoned me, but I'm not sure I entirely, truly understood, back then, why she had to be away so late in the day, and sometimes weekends. Adults and their jobs were foreign concepts.

Mrs. Gilmore raised her chin and said, "All right, then, Rebecca. You can help, but you must do whatever I say. You may touch nothing without my permission, is that understood?"

"Yes ma'am," I said, assuming she meant the rolling pin, which might break if I dropped it, or the ovens.

She handed me a red and white gingham-checked apron that was so long on me, it almost hit the floor. And so began my gingerbread-baking apprenticeship.

Mrs. Gilmore soon learned that I was truly interested in baking as well as being an excellent sous chef, listening carefully to her instructions, asking for clarification when I didn't understand or I wanted her approval over something I'd done.

Early on, she taught me how to run the Kitchenaid mixer, and tasked me with sliding trays into and out of the oven, the latter carefully placed on quilted potholders. Then she entrusted me with easing the cookies from the trays to the cooling racks.

Each year, she gave me a little more responsibility, until I was fifteen and she actually shared her secret recipe with me.

By then I was almost single-handedly doing the decorating, sitting at her kitchen table on a black pleather-and-chrome chair, surrounded by icings and colored sugar and sprinkles and those tiny silver-colored balls.

Mrs. Gilmore had a huge assortment of cookie cutters. Gingerbread men (and women), trees, teddy bears. Six-pointed stars for the Jewish community. Cottages (if the chimney broke off, we'd trim off the eaves as well and decorate the remaining rectangles as gift boxes). Sleighs, snowmen, candy canes, stockings, and simple round ones to be decorated as ornaments

She eschewed reindeer (the horns were too delicate) and angels (ditto the halos). Santas were dicey, thanks to his hat, but sometimes we could pull a few of those off if we felt adventurous.

Also, there were custom cookies like those six-pointed stars. Fire engines for the brave men and women who risked their lives to save our homes. Cars for her mechanic's shop. Open books for the library folks.

Then came the year I turned sixteen. My birthday was early in the year, and like many of my friends I took driver's ed as soon as I was allowed. By the time Thanksgiving rolled around, I was legal to drive by myself until eleven p.m.

Obviously, by that point it had been years since I *had* to spend afternoons and weekends at Mrs. Gilmore's, and during the school year I often didn't see her for a few months at a stretch until the holidays (in the summer I now volunteered at the library book sale, though). Occasionally she invited me over to teach me some new baking technique, and of course I was practicing at home, perfecting my lemon bars and chocolate chip cookies and oatmeal-coconut confections to near-obsession.

Sugar was becoming part of my veins, I swear. And I could tease out a cookie recipe's ingredients by smell (although not the proportions. But by then I was experimenting and creating my own).

Baking the gingerbread cookies—mixing, cutting, baking, decorating—took the bulk of Mrs. Gilmore's time for a solid two months. But there was another time consideration: how long it took to *deliver* those ginger-redolent gift tins.

By this point, although I admittedly loved working with Mrs. Gilmore in the kitchen, I didn't need much more instruction from her. So when she asked me to take over delivery, I agreed. It was a small way I could pay her back for the years of education.

By this point, I hadn't realized how little I knew about Mrs. Gilmore.

And that almost ended me.

On December twenty-first, a Friday, I did an afternoon delivery run to catch people at the offices that would be shutting down before Christmas. (Why make employees come in on Monday only to give them Tuesday and days after off?)

On December twenty-third, a knock sounded at Mrs. Gilmore's door.

The police.

They were looking for me.

The older one, Officer Hahn, had a bit of gray at his temples, and lines around his brown eyes. He was lean and fit, and he didn't smile. The younger one, Officer Gregory, wore her blond hair in a tight bun. Her blue eyes didn't smile, either.

In hindsight, they should have made sure my mother was there. Had she known what was going on without her consent, she would have sued the department six ways to Sunday. Maybe they thought Mrs. Gilmore's presence was enough.

Surely they hadn't suspected me, not really. I was the good kid: bookworm, got good grades, on the school newspaper staff and in the library club, the latter two to which I often brought baked goods while we worked after school.

We sat across from one another in Mrs. Gilmore's living room, me in a turquoise club chair and Mrs. Gilmore in the matching one, separated by a round, marble-topped table bearing a marble-based lamp, and the officers on the nubbly turquoise sofa where I'd spent hours in other worlds.

I was firmly in this world right now, no matter how much I wished otherwise.

Officer Hahn confirmed my name, my address, and the fact that I'd delivered cookies on Friday.

The ginger and sugar scents that permeated the warm air made my stomach roiled as if I'd eaten dough and contracted salmonella from the raw eggs.

"You delivered cookies to Dr. Bronson's office," Officer Hahn said, looking at his small flip-top notebook. "At three thirty-seven PM."

"That sounds about right," I said. "I didn't look at the exact time, but yes, around then."

"Including a tin of cookies labeled for Amy Yarbrough."

I shook my head. "Who?"

The officers exchanged glances. "Amy Yarbrough," Officer Hahn repeated. "A nurse at Dr. Bronson's office."

"Um, maybe?" I shrugged. "I didn't look at the box. There were several tins inside. Why?"

Another glance between them. This time, it was Officer Gregory who spoke. She leaned forward as if we were confidantes.

"Amy Yarbrough was poisoned," she said. Her voice was light, but her words were heavy and dark. "She would have died if Dr. Bronson hadn't recognized the symptoms and administered an antidote before the ambulance got there."

My mouth was dry, as if I'd packed it with flour. I struggled to find saliva so I could speak. "Poisoned?" I managed. "From...from the cookies?"

"As near as we can tell, yes," Officer Gregory said. She clasped her hands together. "Did you make the cookies, Rebecca?"

My mind whirled. I hadn't packed the tins, but I had been helping Mrs. Gilmore with the baking during the week, so it was possible the cookies came from a batch I'd handled.

But I hadn't put anything poisonous in the cookies.

I didn't know Amy Yarbrough. Had never heard her name until just now. Had never been to Dr. Bronson's office before the delivery.

I had no way to prove any of those things.

My body, my head, felt light. Was this what it felt like before you passed out? I didn't know how to form words. My heart raced and I was having trouble breathing. I was the good kid. I...

I glanced over at Mrs. Gilmore. Not that I thought she could save me; I suppose I wanted to see a familiar face, one that didn't seem to be accusing me.

Above her bleeding lipstick, her lip shone with sweat. Sweat darkened the pits of her loose white button-down shirt, too. The fabric was heavy enough that it wasn't entirely noticeable that she wasn't wearing a bra. When I'd figured that out, I'd been shocked. I couldn't imagine my mother going braless. As far as I knew, she wore one when she slept.

Softly, she said, "Rebecca, did you deliver the cookies to the right places?"

My knee-jerk reaction was to say yes, of course I did. I was always ultra-careful to do so, because some were custom.

But then I remembered. My guilty, hasty secret because I'd been running late on Friday, eager to get to the school newspaper's holiday party.

The sticky notes had fallen off a couple of the tins in one box. I was sure I'd replaced them correctly.

I said as much, my voice shaking with confusion and terror.

Mrs. Gilmore stood, walked over to the side of my chair, and placed one hand on the back.

"I'm the one you should be talking to, officers," she said. "Rebecca is completely innocent."

"If you're lying to protect—" Officer Hahn began.

"I am not," Mrs. Gilmore said. "I can tell you the exact poison I used, and why, but I will not do so in front of Rebecca. I will answer all of your questions at the station. To make it clear, I am confessing to the poisoning of Amy Yarbrough, and Rebecca Cavanaugh had no knowledge of it."

I wasn't sure what to do after they took Mrs. Gilmore away.

I cleaned the kitchen, as she'd taught me to. I threw away the finished cookies, the ones that had burned in the oven, the dough in the Kitchenaid stainless steel mixer bowl, and the cookies we'd cut out that were waiting for baking.

Then I went home, to a house that sometimes seemed less inviting that Mrs. Gilmore's. Not anymore.

I NEVER WENT BACK, AND I NEVER SAW MRS. GILMORE again in person. I never got to say...well, I'm not sure what I would have said. Except thank you. She had kept her secret for years, but she had confessed to protect me.

She had intended to poison the receptionist at Dr. Bronson's office, who had given her a hard time about scheduling appointments. The office rule was that you had to confirm your appointment the day before or they canceled the appointment. Mrs. Gilmore thought that was ridiculous, as she had never missed an appointment in her life and if she knew she would, she would call immediately.

Poisoning someone over something like would seem like overkill if the rest of the truth hadn't come out. And most people weren't convinced it was all of the truth.

Every year, apparently, Mrs. Gilmore had targeted someone who had wronged her that year, in her opinion. Because the deaths frequently looked accidental, nobody had run a toxicology report and nobody had made the connection until now.

The hairdresser who died of smoke inhalation when her house caught on fire thanks to untended candles. The mechanic who slid off the road on his way home, crumpling his car in a ditch. The woman on the library association who fell asleep in the bath, a wine glass nearby.

How many more? And should I have known?

Mrs. Gilmore never let me eat the batter (I assumed the egg/salmonella thing) or taste the cookies, even the broken-off bits, except for the ones she gave me to take home.

When it occurred to me that she could have targeted my mother, I threw up.

Because I was a minor—and because my mother blew an expected gasket over the fact that I was questioned without her knowledge—my name was left out of the papers and even the court transcript. (The police had, in fact, called my mother beforehand, but she hadn't answered because she'd been in court, ironically. Going ahead without her knowledge or consent was their very big mistake.)

Of course word got around via the hushed gossip network anyway. I graduated a year early, got my associates in business and my certificate in food safety, and moved across the country to open my boutique cookie shop. When my mom retired, she moved to live near me.

My life is good. I love my work, I love my city and my book-filled house, I have great friends and I'm the head of the local library association.

So no, I don't make gingerbread.

Please stop asking me why.

STUPID GAMES

Brittani Menchin yanked open the door to the girls' bathroom, but a few steps in, she froze. And not because of the faint pee smell that meant the space hadn't been cleaned yet. The door easing shut behind her made a little whine, and the third sink on the end dripped like it always did, no matter how many times the janitor tried to fix it, but she'd heard another noise, too.

The bathroom should have been empty. School had been over for two hours, but she'd had an extra band practice—the concert was a week from Saturday—and then she'd stayed behind to help Mr. Wilke stack the chairs. Plus this bathroom was in the back of the school, where no one came unless they had a music class or were in the audiovisual club or some other nonpopular afterschool hobby.

"Hello?" she said. The hollow space made her voice sound strange, distant, as it bounced over the small tan tiles on the floor and the larger beige tiles that covered the bottom half of the walls. To her left were three white sinks, and beyond them, three stalls with metal walls and doors, a shade of pale brown that didn't match the floor or wall tiles.

There was no response, but the lack of sound felt like someone was holding their breath, hoping she'd go away. Brittani clutched the strap of her backpack where it dug into her shoulder. She'd give the person one more chance before she bent down to look for feet.

"Is anybody there? Are you okay?"

For a moment, that silent not-a-silence continued, but then a small voice, tight with tears, said "Britt, is that you?"

It took her another moment to process the voice. "Char?"

Charlotte Dunn had been her best friend for as long as she could remember...until they hit high school. Before that, they'd been happily nerdy together, to the point that in fifth grade, they'd learned a simple substitution cipher and spent the year sending coded messages to each other.

Things had started to change in eighth grade. That was when Brittani's growth spurt started and she'd shot up, as her father put it, like a beanpole. (Because that's supportive attitude. Thanks, Dad.) Meanwhile, Charlotte developed curves.

By ninth grade, Charlotte was officially one of the beautiful girls, blond and perky, with a jaunty swing in her step, and the popular girls had swarmed around her, cutting her away from Brittani.

Brittani, who by now—the autumn of their junior year—had attained what seemed to be her final height (fingers crossed): five-foot-eleven-and-three-quarters.

Charlotte's abandonment of Brittani, combined with her defection to the clique side, had hurt. A lot. Brittani had mostly gotten over it, bonding with the music geeks and the computer nerds.

Key word: mostly. But hearing Charlotte sounding so alone and distressed sent her into Help mode.

"Yeah, it's me. You okay?" Brittani repeated.

"Yes, I'm fi—no. No, I'm not okay."

There was a hitch in Charlotte's voice, the sound she

made when she was desperately trying not to cry. Brittani remembered it from the night Charlotte found out her parents were getting divorced, and the day her dog, Stan von Weinerstan, died.

The voice came from the handicapped stall, the one at the far end. When Brittani got to the door, it swung inward.

Charlotte was huddled on the floor, arms wrapped around her knees. Her face was red and blotchy—if there was such as thing as a non-ugly cry outside of Hollywood, Brittani had certainly never seen it—her eyes were puffy, and the crown of her long, straight ponytail, which smelled like coconut, was poofed up as if it had rubbed against the wall behind her.

Charlotte's hair was never messy.

Brittani crouched down next to her former friend. Even though this was the biggest stall, her jean-clad knees still brushed against the side of the cold porcelain toilet.

That's when she saw the blood.

Charlotte was wearing her cheerleading uniform (of course she'd become a cheerleader): a royal blue knit top with the school logo swoosh in red and white, and a matching blue, ultra short skirt trimmed in red. Her left kneesock was pushed down as far as it would go against her white cheer sneaker. Three thin, parallel scratches ran from her inner ankle to the top of the side of her calf, each oozing a crimson string of beads. Near her knee, the blood was smeared, and there was a corresponding dark smear on Charlotte's forearm.

That was when Brittani noticed the open safety pin Charlotte held loosely between her fingers.

"Oh honey," Brittani said. "Let's get you cleaned up, okay?"

Tears welled in Charlotte's eyes, but she sort of hiccupped and then nodded wordlessly.

Brittani went out and grabbed a handful of paper towels, holding some under a faucet, then wringing them out. She came back and crouched again, and dabbed at Charlotte's leg with the wet paper. Charlotte didn't flinch or make a noise. Brittani rummaged in her backpack, which she'd left on the floor in the stall, until she found some electrical tape (which she carried because, well, you never know when you might need some), and taped a piece of dry towel on Charlotte's calf.

Charlotte dropped the safety pin and pulled her sock up over the makeshift bandage with shaking hands, then wiped her arm clean with a wet towel. Brittani picked up the pin, closed it, and tucked it in her jeans so nobody would accidentally hurt themselves with it.

"Let me pee real quick, and then we'll get you home," Brittani said. Charlotte nodded. Brittani dashed into the next stall and did her business as fast as she could, because she didn't want Charlotte to run off. Something was wrong, and no matter what their friendship was like now—if they even *had* something approaching a friendship—Charlotte was cutting herself, and she needed help.

WALKING INTO THE DUNN HOUSE FELT LIKE WALKING INTO a strange and disconcerting dream. A place she knew and yet didn't know, initially comforting but ultimately leaving her feeling uneasy.

Leaving their shoes on the white wooden rack by the front door—that was familiar. The walls still had the white wainscoting on the bottom half, and Brittani flashed on the memory of them as kids, running in the circle from the front hall, through the parlor, through the living room, through the wainscoting to spin themselves around each corner, parkour style, shrieking with laugher the whole time. Mrs. Dunn would say "Don't leave your grubby fingerprints all over my clean walls," but there wasn't much heat behind it. Although it was always clean by the next time their grubby hands reached out.

The walls above the wainscoting, however, were no longer pale peach, but trendy buttercup yellow, and the area rugs had all been changed out. In the kitchen, the layout was the same, but now the cabinets and everything else were white, accented with stainless steel appliances and pale grey granite countertops. Everything still smelled like bleach and dish-washing detergent.

The familiar/not-familiar was so strong that when Charlotte said, "Would you like something to drink?" Brittani automatically reached to open the cabinet where she knew the glasses were.

Then she drew her hand back, uncomfortable. This was no longer her second home. Now she felt like a guest, awkward, unsure where to sit or put her hands.

"Iced tea would be great, if you have any."

Charlotte didn't seem to notice her discomfort. "Here you go. How about something to eat?"

"Whatever you're having," Brittani said.

"I'm fine with this," Charlotte said, lifting the glass of water she'd poured for herself.

That's when she noticed—or maybe finally processed—how thin Charlotte was. Oh, the curves were still there, because you can't change the bone structure of your hips, and it was also possible Charlotte was wearing a padded bra. But her wrists seemed fragile, and her face was drawn.

"Yeah, I'm fine, too," Brittani said, and they went up to Charlotte's room.

There, gone were the dark plaid, woven bedspread and the posters of the Avengers and Harry Potter and Merida from *Brave*. Now it looked as though *pink* had exploded, from the frilly bedspread to the new vanity covered with makeup.

In some ways, it seemed like a little girl's room, as if Charlotte had regressed.

Charlotte plopped onto the bed and stripped off her socks. "Make yourself at home," she told Brittani as she went into the attached bathroom (also very pink).

Brittani sat, somewhat gingerly, at the foot of the bed, setting her backpack next to her. The bedspread had insets of white eyelet fabric, making the cover feel rough, not welcoming.

The inside of the half-open bathroom door had a mirror on it, and she could see Charlotte's reflection as Charlotte rested one foot on the toilet lid and peeled off the makeshift bandage on her calf. When she opened the medicine cabinet for supplies, Brittani noticed several boxes of Band-Aids.

She felt a cold flush of concern. Nobody needed five boxes of Band-Aids...unless Charlotte's cutting problem was worse than she thought.

Charlotte poured hydrogen peroxide over her leg, and Brittani heard her hiss of pain. Then Charlotte came back and plopped on the bed. She leaned back against the mountain of pillows and began sticking Band-Aids up her leg. Brittani saw a few pale scars on Charlotte's other leg, but that was it. Of course, her arms were covered by her cheerleading sweater, and if she was likely to cut anywhere else, well, Brittani had tuned out the health class movie because she hadn't thought it concerned her.

Charlotte finished, and seemed to remember Brittani was still there. She took a sip of water and put the glass back down on her nightstand, next to her phone, which was decorated with a pink case with rhinestones on it.

"Um," Charlotte said, not meeting Brittani's eyes. "Thanks for bringing me home."

"It's okay," Brittani said. She drew her feet up onto the

bed, tucking them beneath her thighs. "What's going on, Char? What's wrong?"

"Nothing...nothing. I..." Charlotte picked up her phone but didn't turn it on. Instead she turned over and then back again, and sort of fiddled with it, as if she needed to do something with her hands.

Brittani knew she could accept that and walk out. This wasn't her problem.

But it was. Just because she didn't recognize this carnation riot of a room and barely recognized the girl in front of her, well, you don't just walk away from someone who's obviously in distress.

Instead she leaned forward and put a hand on Charlotte's bare knee and said, "Char...?" in a tone that was half-comfort, half-question.

"Oh God, it's just so *stupid*." Charlotte's pretty face crumpled, and her blue-grey eyes brimmed with tears. She'd splashed water on her face, and her mascara was still smudged around her eyes. "It's just..." She took a breath, smoothed out her features. Girding her loins, as they say. "Okay. So, there's this...stupid game that people play at parties. You know, parties that people like Aaron and Joshua and Sasha and Alexis throw."

"Actually, I don't know," Brittani said, trying to keep the sarcasm out of her voice. The kids Charlotte listed were in the In Crowd, not the band geeks and computer nerds.

"I'm sorry," Charlotte said, her cheeks flushing. It was as if for a moment she'd forgotten they weren't still friends. "Their parents don't really monitor the parties—hell, Alexis has the pool house to herself, and the only adult that ever goes in there is the maid, and Alexis pays her really well to get rid of the empties and not say anything. Honestly, though, Britt, I've never been to any of them. I've just heard about them."

Brittani shook her head. "It's okay," she said for what felt like the thousandth time. "Go on. There's a stupid game?"

"Yeah. Everybody takes a sticker with a number on it from a bowl—one bowl for girls, one bowl for boys. Nobody knows anybody else's number."

"Then they pair up and neck?" Brittani said.

"No. Well, that happens later. Each person goes into the bathroom and takes a picture with the sticker." Charlotte took another deep breath. "The girls put the sticker here—" she indicated her breastbone "—and take a picture of their boobs. Naked. Nothing else identifying in the picture. The boys take a picture of their...penises. Then they put the pictures on a computer screen and the boys have to guess who the girls are and the girls have to guess who the boys are."

"Whoa, whoa, *whoa.*" Brittani waved her hands in the air. "Are you *shitting* me? *That's* what you people do for *fun?*"

It was the wrong thing to say—she'd just been too shocked to process everything and censor herself—and Charlotte's floodgates opened again.

"I *know*," she said between sobs. "I *told* you it was stupid."

"So everybody has pictures of their naked boobs and peens on their phones?" Brittani asked. "And on a computer?"

"No," Charlotte said. "It's just one phone, used just for this, and they delete the pictures off the phone and the laptop afterwards."

"You know nothing is ever really deleted," Brittani said. "Anybody with half a brain could access the files, and then you're talking porn—underage porn. Aaron is over eighteen, and so is Sasha, but the rest of you aren't and eighteen is the age of consent in California. Did you fail the Health test on all this? And what if someone sends them out? Sexting is a crime—and do you want the whole school to see your boobs, Char? The whole world? Seriously?"

"No…" Charlotte's voice was barely audible. "I haven't done it. Not yet, anyway. My mom wouldn't let me go to any unchaperoned parties. Everyone knew it, and they understood my mom and stepdad keep close tabs on me. But when I turned seventeen, my parents told me they trusted me, that I could have more independence."

Brittani shrugged. "So don't tell your friends."

Charlotte sighed. "Too late. My mom told the girls when I hosted an after-cheer-practice party. The next party is at Alexis's, and Mom thinks Alexis is a lovely girl."

She said the last phrase in such a perfect imitation of her mother that it choked a laugh out of Brittani. But only for a moment.

"So just don't go," Brittani said. "Or tell them you don't want to play the game."

Charlotte shook her head so violently, her ponytail whipped back and forth enough that Brittani could smell the coconut again. "You don't understand. If that happens…they'll all think I'm a wuss and…and they probably won't want to hang out with me anymore. I don't want to not have any friends." Her voice sounded very small.

Brittani wanted to say *I'm still your friend*, but she didn't. She couldn't. All the pain of Charlotte's rejection rose up and blocked the words in her throat.

Charlotte would have to earn that trust again. If she wanted to.

If Brittani wanted her to.

But that didn't mean Brittani didn't still sympathize. Plus she was glad Charlotte wasn't a *complete* idiot and knew better than to want to go along with the ridiculous game.

Dumbasses.

"Well, then, you're kinda screwed," Brittani said. "I won't tell anyone—but it's your funeral if those photos get out. Unless…" Her thoughts raced and tumbled. Spy movies and geek trivia and a whole mess of other stuff whiffed through her brain, too fast for her to grab onto any of it.

"Unless?" Charlotte asked, leaning forward.

"Unless we find a way to shut the whole thing down. Scare everyone into finding another way to be complete mindless idiots. When's the party?"

"Halloween."

Brittani groaned. That was just two weeks away.

"We can't just steal the laptop and phone," she said. "There's no way of knowing if the pictures have been copied elsewhere."

"I know," Charlotte moaned, her voice nasally from all the crying. "I tried to tell them that, but the girls just brushed it off and the guys looked at me like I didn't understand computers."

Brittani stopped herself right before *And yet you hang out with them* popped out of her mouth.

"Okay," she said. "Let me think about this and get back to you. In the meantime...try not to hurt yourself, okay? It's not worth it."

Charlotte pressed her lips together. "It's like...the only time I don't feel anything. All I feel is that pain."

Brittani pointed at Charlotte's rhinestone phone. "If you feel like you need to do it, *call me*."

BRITTANI FELT PRETTY SMUG WHEN SHE HAMMERED OUT the details of her solution. She met up with Charlotte at Charlotte's house again, because she didn't want to bring Charlotte over and have her mom treat Charlotte like she was Brittani's friend again. Brittani wasn't sure how things would shake out after this little adventure.

On one hand, it was kind of the like old days, with their

coded messages and riding bikes around pretending to be spies (or sometimes superheroes). On the other hand, Charlotte was still maintaining her friendships, and frequently brought up things Brittani had no clue about or didn't care about, or both. Like fashion, and Kardashians. Or, God forbid, Kardashian fashion.

Brittani had her laptop open on Char's uncomfortable but no doubt trendy bedspread.

"So I created a fake website," she explained. "It's an html file that you double-click on. It's not attached to the Internet, though, so none of this will go beyond whoever's laptop they're using."

Charlotte looked blank.

"Fake website," Brittani repeated. "Not online. Just on this thumb drive." She held up a tiny drive, just a little bigger than her fingernail. When it was inserted into the port on the computer, it was practically invisible. "To load the fake website onto their laptop."

She had written a script that would pick all the photos out of whatever folder they stored that night's pictures in, and display them on the fake webpage.

"Here's the thing, though," Brittani went on. "You have to do this. I'll show you the exact things to click; I made it as simple as possible."

"What?" Char's eyes widened. "Why can't you do it?"

Brittani snorted. "I'm not invited to the party."

"But you can go with me," Charlotte said.

"I'm pretty sure your friends don't want me there."

"You'd be surprised," Charlotte said. "They're kind of impressed by you. How you don't give a rat's ass about what anyone thinks about you, how you can be smart and pretty and talented all at once, how you've got your own fashion style."

Brittani had thought her fashion style was *things I can find that are actually long enough*, but it was nice to know that it was working. Somehow. She didn't care about fashion, but she did try to look like she meant to wear the outfit she'd cobbled together.

"How you've got it all together," Charlotte went on. "And some of the guys...they think you're pretty hot."

Brittani raised her eyebrows. Wha—?

"They do. They call you 'Legs'," Charlotte said. "As in, they want to follow those long luscious legs all the way up, or they'd like those legs wrapped around their necks."

"Jesus," Brittani said. "If I wasn't so incredibly outraged at how offensive that is, I might be flattered. Let me tell you, that makes me want to go to the party even less that I did before—when before I didn't want to go at all. But if you think nobody will care that I'm there, it does make more sense for me to do this."

"Thank you," Charlotte breathed, and leaned over and hugged her. Brittani froze, then patted her on the arm, not yet willing to commit.

"Wait," Charlotte said. "This happens *after* we all take our pictures, right? I don't want to do that—I don't want everybody looking at my breasts." She hunched over, as if trying to hide them—even though she was fully dressed, wearing a chunky ribbed sweater that was black at the top but faded down to white at the bottom.

"I thought of that, too," Brittani said, "and thank goodness, because neither do I." As in, oh *hell* no. "Thank God it's Halloween season. I found fake boobs online that are pretty realistic." She called up the gag prosthetics website, and they both looked at it from sideways glances. Disturbing. "We'll strap them on, stick our stickers on them, and take the pictures that way."

They weren't cheap, but Brittani had a credit card because she did online eBay selling for people as her part-time job.

She'd already been planning to buy one for Charlotte, and hit her up for the money later. No sense stressing her out even more; she'd feel better after they succeeded.

They had to succeed. Failure was not an option.

BRITTANI'S PARENTS DIDN'T QUESTION THE PARTY THING, especially when she told them she was going because Charlotte had asked her to come for moral support. "Boy troubles," she told them, because it wasn't really a lie, and then she promised not to drink, but if she did, she'd call them for a ride home.

For the costume party, she dressed as Ripley, Sigourney Weaver's character from the *Alien* movies: dark grey utilitarian jumpsuit over a white T-shirt that nobody, *nobody*, was going to see more than the collar of; black Doc Martens; and a super-soaker in place of the big gun, because she didn't want anybody to mistake it for a real automatic weapon. There was too much of that crazy in the world already.

The jumpsuit was one she picked up at a local uniform store. Because of her height, she could shop in the men's section—which meant it was baggy enough for her comfort. She didn't mind wearing tighter clothes normally, but at this party, with these people? Not a chance.

She'd also added a canvas messenger bag, which wasn't part of the original costume, but served as her purse.

Charlotte wore her cheerleading uniform, but had the good sense to go with full zombie makeup. It looked as though her cheek had been ripped open and there was a gaping bite mark on her neck. Brittani was impressed. That vanity in Charlotte's bedroom and all that makeup had been put to good use.

"You look disgusting," she said.

"Thank you," Charlotte said with a sunny smile, which made her look even more disturbing, and shook the cute coffin purse she carried. It didn't go with her outfit, but it did go with Halloween, at least.

It was just big enough to hold her fake boobs.

The party was at Alexis's pool house. When Brittani and Charlotte got out of the car, they could already hear the throbbing bass that would eventually cause permanent hearing loss, and a few voices heartily singing along. They were so off-key that Brittani couldn't even figure out the song. It made her want to bash them with her French horn.

(The band concert had been the previous night, and had gone well. Charlotte had even come, much to Brittani's surprise, although they hadn't had the chance to talk.)

The lights in the pool glowed red, making the pool itself a chlorine-scented bloodbath. Black spindly Halloween trees dotted with tiny LED lights lined the path, and foam gravestones were scattered in various spots on the lawn, along with a few gargoyles the size of large dogs. (Wrong Sigourney Weaver movie, oh well.) Ottoman-sized black cauldrons spewed a wispy fog, and six hand-holding ghostly figures danced in a circle.

The pool house was a one-story building, with a wall of glass doors that opened up and slid back to allow access to the pool. Clearly no expense had been spared; it looked as though Martha Stewart had exploded. Candelabrums, flying bats, full-height mirrors that reflected you and someone ethereal behind you. A life-sized witch cackled and twitched.

The main room smelled of pot and spilled beer. The bulbs in the various lamps had been changed out to colored ones, so the place was dim, and the hues were all wrong. Everything looked sort of pukey brown, and Brittani couldn't see much in the enforced gloom. Just the shapes of furniture covered with people, really, until you got close.

Fortunately or unfortunately, the partygoers had been waiting for Charlotte and Brittani's arrival to really get the party started. A cheer rose when the two of them were spotted.

Brittani's mouth had already been dry, and now her stomach bounced around more than the notes in a complex Wagner piece. (The band instructor, Mr. Wilke, was a big Wagner fan.) Someone pressed a drink into her hand, and she pretended to take a sip. She had a bottle of water in her bag; there was no way she was drinking *anything* here.

The bowls were passed; the numbered stickers were chosen. Brittani and Charlotte would go last, because they were new, which added to Brittani's tension. She guessed it was to get her and Charlotte liquored up a bit so they wouldn't chicken out.

She saw Charlotte take a swallow her beer, and shook her head just a tiny bit at her friend. Charlotte, thankfully, saw the motion and understood, because she poured out some of the drink into a potted plant, then took a big fake swig.

Then it was Brittani's turn. She went into the bathroom, which had a black marble countertop and black walls, and one of those above-the-counter flat sinks with a faucet that spilled the water out like a mini-waterfall.

She couldn't believe she was doing this.

She realized she hadn't really thought her costume through when she discovered how long it took to wiggle out of the top and strip off the undershirt and bra. She pulled the rubbery latex fake boobs out of her bag and strapped them on, then pressed at the edges, trying to smooth them against her skin. She didn't have time for the special makeup to blend the edges together; she just had to hope for the best. She stuck the sticker in between and took a deep breath.

Cell phones didn't take great photos anyway, and she turned off the brighter lights above the sink before she took the shot, so there would be more shadows. She adjusted the screen so it was getting only her chest and a bit of her ribcage, but not the jumpsuit where it bunched around her waist.

She checked the phone. At least in the small version, the boobs weren't obviously fake.

Someone pounded on the door. "Almost done!" she called.

Putting her clothes back on was even harder; her skin was sticky with sweat. She yanked and tugged at the jumpsuit, and in the mirror she saw her face looked shiny. She blotted it with a black towel, leaving streaks of pale makeup.

When she came out, she handed off the phone to Charlotte, her heart pounding from the adrenaline and stress, her hands clammy. She wandered over near the laptop, a cheap Acer. To her relief, she saw the USB cable that they obviously used to attach the phone to the computer to transfer the pictures. At least they weren't doing it wirelessly.

If they were, there'd be no way to make sure the pictures never got out. So that was a small gift.

Charlotte emerged from the bathroom, her zombie makeup smudged and fake blood on the collar of her cheerleading top. Because that had been even harder to get out of than Brittani's jumpsuit. Her eyes were a little glassy, and Brittani hoped it wasn't from something in the little bit she'd had to drink.

Or that she wasn't going to pass out or something. Brittani still needed her for the plan to work.

Aaron, who was tall and blond and crewcutted and a big-shouldered football player (Brittani didn't know what position he played, because her only experience at football games was playing in the marching band at halftime and then getting the hell out of there), took the phone from Charlotte. He was dressed as Kristoff from *Frozen*, as near as Brittani could tell, in an all-black outfit with a burgundy sash around his waist. Despite the fact that he was swaying a little on his feet, he deftly connected the phone to the laptop and transferred the pictures.

There was cheering, and a bottle of rum was passed around, splashed into people's cups. Brittani was glad she'd taken a swig of her safe water in the bathroom, because even with all the doors open, the room was feeling pretty hot, and her T-shirt was sticking to her back.

The pictures came up. First the boobs, not surprisingly. There was much hooting and hollering and jostling as everyone crowded in to see the display and guess whose hooters.

That was the name of the game: Whose Hooters. Soon to be followed by Pick the Dick.

Seriously.

Brittani let herself be jostled to the front. She felt a pang of guilt for blocking other people's view before she reminded herself of the reason she needed to be there. This was not the time to be self-conscious about her height.

She let out a long breath when the fake boobs weren't noticed. The graininess of the pictures helped, along with the chemically modified state of the viewers. The only reason she could tell was that she knew what she was looking for.

Then, Charlotte screamed. She had a scream that Hollywood would have envied, because it pierced over the noise like an icepick into an eyeball.

When everyone turned, Brittani jammed the tiny thumb drive into another USB port on the laptop. The few quick clicks seemed to take a lifetime, and the thought consumed her that she had no idea what to do if she were caught.

"I'm sorry," Charlotte was saying, swaying a little into Joshua's arms. Damn, her acting wasn't too shabby, either. "I thought I saw a spider."

"You mean like this one?" someone shouted, and tossed a

pie-pan-sized fake hairy spider into the crowd. Cue lots and lots more screaming. Brittani did all she could not to scream herself. She *loathed* spiders. They were the worst part of Halloween.

The folder opened and the html file loaded, and the script ran, pulling up the photos.

Her turn.

"Guys? Guys! HEY WHAT THE FUCK GUYS!"

Now everyone turned in her direction. It was disconcerting. She wasn't used to being that much the focus of attention of so many eyes. So many potentially unfriendly eyes.

She pointed a shaking finger at the screen, hoping her acting was half as good as Charlotte's. "The pictures—they're up on a website."

Her faux website was good—really good. It even included people's first names. She hadn't been able to match up boobs and dicks with names ahead of time, though; she'd relied on the shock factor to keep anyone from noticing.

There was expected mayhem and horror, shouting and panic. But Brittani was still surprised when everyone turned to her for help. They knew she was a computer geek—and they knew they needed her help.

Now was not the time to revel in the headiness of it all.

"We have to destroy the evidence," she said. "Make sure it doesn't get traced back to us. Anybody could have those first names."

Nobody stopped her when she picked up the laptop and still-attached phone, pushed her way through the crowd, and flung both into the Countess Bathory pool.

At the last second, she remembered to pull her thumb drive out.

A splatter of pool water hit her face, pungent with chlorine, and she thought after a party like this, bleach really was the best solution.

There was a moment of silence (except for the *boomboom-boom* of the music) while everyone watched the laptop slowly drift to the bottom of the pool.

"What now?" someone broke the silence.

"The chlorine will do a lot of damage, but I'd still recommend destroying the hard drive," Brittani said.

"I'll get it!" someone shouted, and a very drunk guy she didn't even recognize threw himself into the pool. She worried about him, even more than the computer, until he resurfaced.

Someone pressed a hammer into her hand. She didn't question it. She just went to town on the computer and the phone, adding the weight of her anger at Charlotte and the whole stupid clique, an anger that she hadn't known she carried.

Or maybe not anger at Charlotte. She'd seen the blood, the scars, on her friend's legs. Nobody should feel that kind of anxiety in high school. Nobody should need to do that.

Through the canvas jumpsuit, the concrete was rough and hard beneath her knees.

Wham. Pieces of plastic shot in all directions, stinging her face, smelling of chlorine.

Wham. Her hand and wrist hurt from the vibration of the hammer hitting electronics sitting on concrete.

Wham. Damn that felt good, though.

"I'll take everything home and dispose of it," she said, and a moment later Alexis pressed a box of Ziploc bags into her hand (because of course a pool house would have them stocked in the kitchen).

"What about the website?" Alexis asked. She was dressed as a female Iron Man, in a formfitting printed suit and a carefully drawn-on goatee. Her straight dark hair was slicked back into a short ponytail. The look was surprisingly accurate, despite her curves.

Brittani's mouth dried. She hadn't thought about how to explain that away.

She punted, hoping everyone was too drunk to realize she was inventing technobabble the likes of which even *Star Trek* writers had never come up with. She was barely aware of what she was even saying.

Charlotte was at her side as Brittani stood, stuffing the Ziplocs into her messenger bag.

"Great party," Brittani said. "Happy Halloween." She turned to Alexis. "Thanks for having me," she said, and she meant it. She didn't care about the It Crowd per se, but it was nice to not be an outcast, even for one night.

Even if the party had been soundly awful.

By the time she'd slid into the driver's seat of the car—her parents' second car, a safe, old blue-green Nissan Sentra that got good gas mileage—she was really shaking, from deep down in her core.

They'd pulled it off.

She shook her head. They really owed her.

Of course, there was always the possibility that the game would continue in some other form, but right now, all she cared about was that it was on hold for now, and Charlotte hadn't experienced the humiliation of sharing a picture of her boobs.

"Thank you," Charlotte said, grabbing Brittani's hand where it rested on the gearshift.

"Couldn't have done it without you," Brittani said.

Charlotte didn't reply, and Brittani realize the words had probably meant more than she'd intended.

"We make a good team," she said, and she wasn't sure if that made it better or worse.

ON MONDAY, SCHOOL WAS WEIRDLY DIFFERENT. Differently weird. People she'd never really talked to before, people she knew by sight but didn't interact with, said hello to her in the halls, raised a hand for a fist-bump, nodded a greeting as she slid into a too-small classroom seat, her knees banging on the underside of the desk and her bridges of her feet pressed against the metal book rack beneath the chair in front of her.

Charlotte ran into her in the hall after third period. "Want to meet me for lunch outside?" she asked over the din of conversation and banging lockers, and Brittani said yes.

It was sunny but cold, with that crisp autumn chill that made you happy to be alive even as you added another layer of clothing. Brittani felt the metal seat of the picnic table ooze cold through her jeans to her butt.

"How are you?" Brittani asked, popping the top on her can of Chef Boyardee ravioli, because nothing said lunch like cold ravioli. She'd been eating it since she was five, and nobody was going to stop her. Even though she'd perfected the art of making ravioli from scratch, cold Chef Boyardee straight from the can was *sacred*.

Charlotte clearly understood what the question meant. "Better," she said. "It's still...it'll still be a struggle," she said. She rubbed her calf beneath her black tights, no doubt running her fingers over the scars she knew lay beneath. "I've got some stuff to figure out. My mom and I are looking for a therapist I can talk to."

Then she grinned the lopsided grin Brittani remembered from when they were kids. "But my association with you has raised my street cred."

"I can't imagine how that's even possible," Brittani said, despite the weird props she'd been given this morning. She'd assumed the attention would fade away well before Christmas vacation.

Charlotte shrugged. "You're different. To them, that makes you mysterious or something. I don't really understand it myself. You're just you. And…" She looked down, pushing her salad around with her plastic fork. "I've missed you," she said finally. "I got all flattered by their attention, and by the time I realized that, you had a new group of friends…"

It was, Brittani realized, a different perspective on what had happened. Charlotte hadn't felt the pain she had. Charlotte hadn't even realized that she'd caused pain. It was like when Charlotte's parents had split up: they'd been too caught up in their own lives to really see how it had affected Char.

But she couldn't help feeling a little hurt. "So we're friends again now?"

Charlotte flushed, the red staining her cheeks in a way that reminded Brittani her friend was human. "I'm just saying…yes, I hope so. I hope we can be."

"Hey, you came to the band concert. That counts for something."

"I've always envied your musical ability."

"Well, you are the most coordinated cheerleader on the field, so that's saying something," Brittani said.

Charlotte laughed. "I'm not sure where that came from. Remember the summer I tried to learn how to waterski?"

Brittani did. It had taken Charlotte all summer. There had been a lot of flailing and splashing. A lot of laughter, too.

She'd missed that. But she also wasn't ready to full-on become besties again, not without caution.

Besides, for all she knew, Charlotte's friends were going to get into another stupid game she'd have to rescue them from.

GIRL WITH A MISSION

In my school, I'm known as The Fixer.

It's a stupid name, which says something not very kind about the average creativity of the student body.

I'd gotten the nickname after I helped my former-and-maybe-again best friend Charlotte, after Charlotte had fallen in with the popular crowd. The idiots had developed the world's stupidest party game, "Whose Hooters?" (and its counterpart, "Pick the Dick"), which involved photos of private parts. You know, what came down to child pornography for high school students, if they'd been caught. I used my computer acumen to make them believe the photos had been leaked to the Internet, and shut down the game.

Now they thought I was brilliant. If I cared, I could practically call myself popular-adjacent.

So when head cheerleader Tara Kildare sat down at my table in the lunch room, I wasn't exactly startled. Just vaguely annoyed.

It was nearly Christmas, which meant white lights wrapped around palm trees and fake pine greenery everywhere. The Santa Ana winds were blowing, the hot winds from hell that made your eyeballs ache. I wasn't much for girly stuff, but when the Santa Anas hit, I bathed in unscented body lotion.

Normally I ate at the tables outside, but the winds had driven me inside, where I huddled in the air conditioned lunch room, an unassuming expanse of a place filled with round tables that seated six, uncomfortable molded-plastic red chairs, and the surprisingly enticing scent of Salisbury steak. From past experience, I knew the mystery meat dish didn't live up to its aroma, and besides, nothing beat Chef Boyardi ravioli cold out of a can. To make my meal more healthy, I'd brought two homemade zucchini bars. Cream cheese frosting or no, they included vegetables, so they counted.

"Brittani," Tara said.

Yes, I hate my name, and especially the spelling of it, but my mother loves it and I can't hurt her feelings. "Tara."

When I'd been in seventh grade—a time when nobody looked their best, Tara had taken it upon herself to walk up to me one day with all the confidence of being one grade ahead of me, curl her lip in a sneer, and announce that I was ugly.

My parents aren't religious people, but they have a strong moral code. My mother espouses what she calls the Bill and Ted Philosophy: "Be excellent to each other." This is why, in seventh grade, I hadn't kicked Tara in the proverbial nuts. However, I also hadn't developed a witty repartee, so I'd just let her flounce off.

This right here was the first time she'd spoken to me in four years. And even now, I could tell she was judging me, as her pale blue eyes took in my auburn hair, which I'd plaited into to braids in deference to the heat.

Still, she reined in her impulse to make a snarky comment, sucked in a breath, and said, "I need your help."

Tara's long black hair was pulled back into a ponytail,

which went well with her cheerleading uniform. But the royal blue knit top with the school logo swoosh in red and white seemed almost baggy on her, and her naturally pale skin had an unhealthy pallor. She was clearly under a lot of stress over something.

Declining her request based on a nasty comment made four years ago would be petty.

"Meet me in my office after school," I said. "Room M102, first door on your left. But remember, I don't change grades, provide tests, or make fake IDs."

Tara actually looked relieved. "Okay," she said. "Um, thanks."

Her gratitude, and the fact that she'd swallowed her pride to approach me, made me wonder just how bad things had to be for Tara to ask for my help. I'd find out soon enough.

***

ROOM M102 WAS THE BAND PRACTICE ROOM (M101 WAS orchestra), and the first door on the left lead to the anteroom where the loaner instruments for kids who couldn't afford their own were stored. Two walls were covered with cheap metal shelving, on which sat black cases with numbers scribbled on them with thick silver Sharpie. On the wall opposite the door was a rack for upright basses, cellos, and trombones.

The 40-watt fluorescent lights all worked on a good day, and the ceiling was low enough that my head almost grazed those lights. My fingers were crossed that at five-foot-eleven-and-three-quarters, I'd reached my final height. Unfortunately, I'm not coordinated enough for basketball nor twig-shaped enough to be a runway model, so thank goodness I have a computer- and math-oriented brain to fall back on.

The small room smelled of slightly rancid valve oil and something I'd rather not think too hard about.

The storage closet was used for assignations among the popular band crowd.

Yes, there was a popular band crowd. Playing a musical instrument looked good on a college application.

No, I had not partaken of the room in such a manner.

Tara was ten minutes late.

"Sorry," she said. "I've never been in this wing before."

Her college application clearly focused on other pursuits, and no one came to the Nerd Wing unless they had a music class or were in the audiovisual club or some other nonpopular afterschool hobby.

I'm enough of a nerd that I help tidy up after band practices so often that Mr. Wilke, the director, gave me a key.

I leaned back against the shelving, my hip near my own French horn, and said, "So, what's wrong?"

Whatever was going to come out of her mouth, what she said next was probably the last thing I was expecting.

"I've been accused of statutory rape."

"Wait. What? You've been...you've been raped?"

"No!" She looked at me as if I were an imbecile, which made me wonder if I have that look on my own face a lot, dealing with her crowd. "*I'm* being accused of statutory rape."

"Look, Tara, I don't get involved in things the police should be handling—"

"Please," she said. I saw the tears brimming in her eyes, and suddenly I knew how hard this must be for her. She looked like Charlotte for a moment, when Char had asked for help over the stupid party game.

"Give me the details," I said, "and then I'll decide."

Because of those weird birthday rules that determine when you can enter kindergarten, Tara was already eighteen, which made her an adult in the eyes of the law. The person she'd slept with was seventeen, and the sex was consensual. Not exactly icky. Like I said, even this storage closet had seen some things. Sex among high school students was far from unusual.

But the other person's parents were up in arms, and wanted to press charges.

I wasn't sure what I could do. Out of curiosity more than anything else, I asked, "Who's the other person?"

Tara looked away. Sank her teeth into an otherwise perfectly manicured cuticle and worried at it.

"Tara?"

Her eyes flicked back to me. "This is confidential, right?"

"Absolutely." And it was. I would never betray someone who'd confided in me.

Still she hesitated, shifting from foot to foot, the muscles in her thighs flexing, while I ran through a mental list of possibilities. Whom had I seen Tara dating? She wasn't someone I'd paid attention to, given any thought to—and we didn't exactly attend a lot of the same functions. Except maybe football games, because of marching band. Thank the gods that was over for the year.

"Tara?" I asked again.

"Chaya. Chaya Gardner." It came out of her in a rush, and she wouldn't meet my gaze.

Oh. Her hesitation became crystal clear.

I knew Chaya. She actually lived down the street from me, and we'd been friends as kids. Not as close as Charlotte and I, but we'd hung out in the way little kids do when they share a neighborhood park.

Not just as kids, really. I'd been to her birthday party last year, a pool party in their backyard, one of a couple dozen teens.

She was Cambodian, if I remembered correctly. Adopted by the Gardners as a baby, after their mission in Southeast Asia. Her three older brothers were the natural-born children of Jill and Frank Gardner, and Chaya had once confided in me that she thought they'd adopted her rather than try for a girl.

I'd had no idea either Chaya or Tara was gay.

"Okay," I said. "I can see why you want to keep this a secret—"

"It's not that," Tara said, and now her pale blue eyes flashed with anger. "I'm not ashamed, and neither is she. It was private. Our close friends knew, but we didn't see the need to advertise our relationship."

They'd been dating for two years. I am clearly not as observant as I'd thought.

Tara laid out the next, now obvious, wrinkle in the problem. The devoutly Mormon Gardners not only had expected their precious baby girl to remain a virgin until marriage, they'd expected a traditional marriage.

Imagine their surprise when they walked in on said precious baby girl with her very female lover.

According to Tara, even though Chaya insisted to her parents that she was a willing participant, they were sure Tara had manipulated Chaya, and they were outraged enough to press charges. They'd met with an attorney, but hadn't gone to the police yet (unless they'd done so today). In the meantime, they'd yanked Chaya out of school.

"Jesus, Tara, I'm so sorry," I said, and I was.

I mean, my parents had no problem with my being a lesbian, and even though we hadn't discussed it, I was pretty sure they knew my sleepovers with my friend Zan weren't platonic. At least nobody had to worry about an accidental pregnancy, you know?

"But I'm not sure what I can do to help," I went on. "Chaya's a minor in the eyes of the law, so it's your word against her parents'."

"Chaya says her parents like you," Tara said. She was twisting a silver puzzle ring around and around on her forefinger. Because she'd lost weight, it was a little big. I'd bet money she'd gotten it from Chaya. "Maybe you could talk to them?"

Parents, in general, did like me. I was smart, polite, and didn't get into trouble. But did that mean I could convince the Gardners to back down from their religious wrath?

I doubted it. But I was willing to try. Tara might be judgmental and bitchy, but she didn't deserve this. And Chaya certainly didn't, either.

I DROPPED MY BACKPACK AT HOME AFTER SCHOOL AND walked a block over to the Gardner's house.

Most of the lawns in the neighborhood were green, in defiance of the drought. A few houses had gardens with native plants instead, succulents and rocks and a dry birdbath or a glass gazing ball on a plinth for decorative interest. The strong, dry winds had blown heavy palm fronds into the street, and I wished I'd grabbed a bottle of water before leaving the house.

The houses themselves were all two-story Mediterranean-style places with red clay tile roofs and stucco siding in some shade of beige, from pinkish-tan to yellowish. Some had brightly tiled entranceways, and most had black iron screen security doors, which allowed you to open the solid inner door and still have a locked door while you let the breeze in.

Not at this time of year, though. All the doors and windows were shut tight, with air conditioning keeping things cool inside.

Chaya herself opened the door, and she wasn't surprised to see me. Tara had texted her that I'd agreed to help.

"I'm so glad to see you!" she said, hugging me. Her dark brown hair was cut in a bob that accentuated her high cheekbones. But her hair looked lanky, as if she hadn't bothered to shower this morning. She was easily half a foot shorter than me, maybe a little more.

Her parents weren't home, but in truth, I'd wanted the chance to talk to Chaya alone, just to get her side of the story.

She led me into the living room to our right, two steps down onto a parquet floor covered with overstuffed furniture upholstered in Black Watch plaid. The vaulted ceiling had dark beams, and a fan in the center that turned at half-speed, keeping the cool air circulating.

The white-painted built-in bookshelves, credenza, and walls were covered with family photos, dating back at least a couple generations. Higher shelves held trophies of various sports.

Mrs. Gardner must have put spaghetti sauce in the slow cooker this morning, because the house smelled like garlic and tomatoes and basil, and my stomach rumbled. Ravioli had been a long time ago.

Thankfully, I'd brought chocolate-chip cookies as a peace offering—I'd been on a baking kick last night, and zucchini bread had been only part of it—so I helped myself to one now, while Chaya brought glasses of water from the kitchen.

"Thanks," I said, gulping down half of the water. I set it down on a sandstone coaster that bore a religious quote.

Chaya confirmed everything Tara had said, while fiddling with a silver puzzle ring on her thumb, confirming my suspicions.

"My parents are *furious*," she said. "I've tried and tried to talk to them...but they've never listened to me, you know?"

I knew. They'd dressed her in frilly pink dresses when she'd wanted to grub about in the sandbox; they'd sent her to ballet and tap lessons and she ditched them for Little League. She was smart, though, so thankfully everyone was happy when it came to school and grades and Student Council—they even stopped protesting about her playing soccer and field hockey.

"It'll be such a relief when I turn eighteen and can get to college," she said. "At least they aren't insisting I go out on a mission. They'd prefer I go to a local college, but I've gotten an early admission decision from UC Santa Barbara."

Far enough that she couldn't commute from home, at least, but a long enough drive that they weren't likely to drop in for a surprise visit too often.

"I feel sick to my stomach about Tara," Chaya went on. "I can't believe they're being so vindictive."

And the law, technically, was on their side.

I'd done a little research on my phone on the bus home. As I understood it, because of how close they were in age, Tara wouldn't be charged with more than a misdemeanor. But that could still mean up to a year in county jail...

Any fair judge wouldn't do more than slap Tara on the wrist.

Call me cynical, but I didn't have a lot of hope for a fair judge. Frank Gardner was a judge himself. He couldn't preside over the proceedings, of course, but he had friends.

I finished my cookie and my water, and got up to pace the room. Chaya followed me, pointing out people in the pictures. Almost all of them were in fancy, off-white shabby-chic frames that made my teeth itch.

The one of her parents in high school was kind of adorable in a parent kind of way. Mom had long, hugely curly blond hair and dark red matte lipstick. Dad wore a tux, but his hair was a shade longer than proper.

"Junior prom," Chaya said. "My parents were high school sweethearts—they'd been dating since eighth grade. Hypocritical, isn't it, that they think Tara and I aren't serious? I mean, yes, I know most high school romances don't last, and we're going to different colleges—if Tara even gets to go to college—so we could meet other people. But that doesn't mean I don't love her now."

There were a lot of photos of Chaya's three older brothers. I vaguely remembered them, all broad-shouldered and blond and sporty. They'd been a little bullying when I was a kid, but not in a truly mean way.

Hang on. In some of the photos, there were four boys. They all looked clearly related. Had Chaya had a brother who died? I didn't remember that, but then, it might be something the family didn't talk about.

"Who's this?" I asked.

"Oh, that's my Uncle Ted," she said. "My grandmother had a surprise kid later in life, you know? He spent summers with us, because he was just a few years older than Gary, my oldest brother."

Made sense. The Gardners weren't the polygamous type of Mormons, but they still had a large extended family. The backdrop of a lot of earlier photos—when Jill and Frank were younger, with their respective families, were clearly not taken in Southern California.

"Augusta, near Atlanta," Chaya said. "Mom and Dad moved here before Gary was born."

I heard the faint rumble of a garage door, and then a distant sound of a door opening.

"They're home," Chaya said, her voice tight with nerves.

Despite my own nerves, the Gardners seemed delighted to see me. Frank looked me up and down, called me a tall drink of water, pumped my hand once, and went off to his man cave or wherever. Jill sat on the edge of the sofa next to me and asked how I'd been.

Her hair was a darker blond, now, and cut in a ubiquitous middle-aged short style that still seemed too old for her. Her navy slacks and sleeveless ivory silk shell were timeless, as was the strand of fat rectangular gold chain links around her neck. She'd gained weight after three children, but she wore it well. Her fingers were heavy with gold and diamond rings.

I hate talking to parents, but I know how to pull it off. I said I'd applied to Stanford, among other universities, but that was my dream, and I wanted to major in computers. I mentioned the school's upcoming winter concert (band, orchestra, chorus). I asked about the market, because she was a real estate agent. I told her how delicious her sauce smelled, and she told me her secret was a tablespoon of brown sugar to cut the acidity of the tomatoes.

When we'd run out of chitchat (thank goodness—it was excruciating, except for the part about the brown sugar, which I filed away for later experimentation), she said, "It's so lovely to see you. You're such a good friend to Chaya."

The clear implication was, I was a good friend because I hadn't deflowered her precious little girl. I tried not to grind my teeth. I already have to wear a night guard.

"I know Chaya and I don't get the chance to hang out a lot," I said, "but she really is a friend."

"And she needs *real friends* right now," Mrs. Gardner said, reaching over and taking Chaya's hand in her own.

Chaya's back was stiff as a board, and I could tell she was doing everything in her power not to snatch her hand out from under her mother's.

"I agree," I said. "She's really stressed out—I'm sure you can see that. She's really worried about what's going to happen. Tara—"

At the very mention of Tara's name, Mrs. Gardner's demeanor changed. Her back went as stiff as Chaya's, and any friendliness fled her face, replaced by a coldness that was kind of terrifying.

"Tara is no longer welcome here, and we will not speak of

that *sinner* in our house," she nearly spat. "I think it's time you headed home, Brittani."

She stood, and I followed suit, feeling like I was a puppet with her strings being tugged.

I hugged Chaya, in part because it might piss off Mrs. Gardner, and headed out into the evening heat, mission definitely not accomplished.

MY PARENTS WERE DUE HOME FROM WORK SOON, AND IT was taco night, which I'd helped prep last night, so dinner wasn't too far away. I poured myself a large glass of iced tea and made myself a plate of Wheat Thins and a hunk of sharp white cheddar anyway, and took it up to my rooms.

Because I'm an only child and our house is ridiculously big for three people, I have a second room attached to my bedroom, which I use as a place to study. Which was useful, because I have multiple computers and a lot of books, plus an electronic keyboard because I'm teaching myself piano. The bare spots on the walls not covered by shelves have posters of Steve Jobs and Bill Gates and Tesla and Einstein and Tony Stark. I have busts of Mozart and Wagner on one desk, and bobbleheads of all The Avengers on another.

I pulled my laptop from my backpack and flopped down lengthwise on the beat-up Victorian divan I'd found on Craigslist for a song (and attacked with a rented steam cleaner before I'd brought it into the house). My feet dangled over the edge, but it was still super-comfortable.

I had homework. I probably should practice my French horn.

But this problem with Tara and Chaya nagged at me.

No. Let's be honest. I was seriously pissed at the Gardners. And I wanted to find a way to keep this from ever getting to the legal system, which would likely screw Tara. She wasn't a friend, but there but for the grace of God, you know?

Plus, be excellent to each other. This wasn't *fair*.

I didn't know how much time we had until the Gardners officially brought charges against Tara. Even though the court stuff would drag on—I knew it wasn't like on TV, when cases get tried days rather than months or even years later—it would mess up Tara's life, and Chaya's.

I didn't open my laptop, because I couldn't even think why. Instead I dropped my head back against a pillow and closed my eyes.

Behind my eyelids I saw the Gardners' living room, looking like a family reunion had exploded.

It was kind of sweet, really. My family was tight, but small. I didn't have a buttload of cousins, a hovering bunch of doting aunts and uncles.

Like the Gardners, we didn't live close to relatives. My parents had ended up, independently, in the area for work, and met through friends. My closest relative was Nonna, my grandmother Lydia, in the Bay Area.

High school sweethearts, Chaya said her parents had been. Junior high, really.

I sat up so fast, I nearly dumped my laptop on the floor. Outside, dusk had fallen, and I could hear noise downstairs: Dad in the kitchen. He usually got home first, started prepping supper.

Was it reasonable to believe that Frank Gardner and his girlfriend, Jill (maiden name currently unknown) had taken and held to a purity pledge? As Mormon and devout as you wanna be, sometimes there's no denying raging teenage hormones, right?

I flopped back down. As if I had some Kilgrave-level

psychic ability to induce them to admit they'd indulged in some serious hanky-panky back in the day.

Still, while I was lying there, I dug my phone out of my jeans pocket and texted Chaya: *What was your mother's maiden name?*

The answer came back almost immediately: *Zabriskie. Why?*

Just a hunch. Oh, and what school did they go to?

Hang on, I'll have to ask.

While I waited, I did my pre-Calc homework.

"Brit?" My mother's voice floated up the stairs. "Dinner, hon."

I went down, because *tacos*. My mother, not from a southwest state, uses store-bought crunchy taco shells and salty Velveeta and tasteless but tactile iceberg lettuce, but damn, it all works somehow.

I'd left my phone upstairs, because we have a rule about no cell phone at the table. When I returned, Chaya had responded.

Jackson High, Augusta.

I cracked my knuckles and called upon my Google-fu.

I found Frank Gardner. Graduated 1993. I found Jill Zabriskie, but no graduation date—her last yearbook photo was 1992, her junior year. I even found that prom photo.

I couldn't find a Jill Zabriskie graduating from any high school in the state that year.

Okay. It was time to go in deeper.

I paused long enough to do the rest of my homework—an outline of an English paper on a novel that changed my life (*The Last Unicorn*), Social Studies reading, Spanish worksheet.

My parents came in at some point and kissed me goodnight and told me not to stay up too late, which they did every night. It was kind of comforting. I knew that if I truly wasn't getting enough sleep on a regular basis, they'd notice, and intervene.

At least, it made me feel good to believe that. It was hard for me to accept that Charlotte had been cutting herself, and her mother hadn't known. Char had finally confessed, and her mother had found her a good therapist, but still.

I went back to my research, after taking out my contacts and rubbing my tired eyes and getting more iced tea.

It was after midnight when I found a piece of information that blew everything out of the water.

I WAS AT THE GARDNERS' HOUSE BRIGHT AND EARLY, standing in front of the garage so when the door went up, I was blocking the two his-and-hers black Lexuses. (Lexi?)

"Brittani," Jill said. Today she wore black pants and a pale pink silk shell with a loose bow around the front. Same jewelry. She was like the cliché of a real estate agent, I swear. "I'm afraid I wasn't clear last night. You're not welcome here right now."

Frank, tall and burly, his mustache neatly trimmed and his cheeks red from his morning shave, made a point of looking at his watch. "I have to get to court, I'm afraid."

Fine.

"You'd rather hear this from me than see it plastered on the Internet," I said, my voice perky, a fake smile crossing my face.

"Brittani," Jill said again. "Yes, we'd be devastated if how Tara manipulated our innocent Chaya made the news. But it will soon; we can't stop that. Justice will prevail. It will only look bad for Tara."

"I'm not talking about that," I said. "I'm talking about

your raging hypocrisy." Still with the smile. My cheeks hurt. Is this what televangelists felt all the time?

They both froze.

"What are you talking about?" Frank asked.

Suddenly, I could hear the Southern in his voice. In Jill's. Something they'd tried to erase. Tried to forget.

Just like this.

I waved a manila envelope. "Chaya's 'uncle' Ted. He's not her uncle, is he?"

Frank looked as though she'd sucked a lemon off the Meyer lemon tree in their backyard. Jill turned white and took a step back, leaning against her car. The look on her face made me almost feel sorry for her.

"He's your son," I persisted anyway, because I was pissed off, because she deserved to have the wound poked. "You got pregnant in high school, which is why you didn't graduate."

"Even if that were true—" Frank began.

It was true. Nice try, Mr. Gardner.

"What this means is that you weren't virgins when you got married, so how, exactly, can you insist that Chaya should be? At least she didn't get pregnant and have to drop out of school and pretend her child was her own mother's, and get her GED, and—"

"Jesus Christ," Frank said, which didn't sound very devout to me. "*Stop it*. Look what you're doing to her."

Rage bubbled up inside of me. "Look what you're doing to *Chaya*," I said. "You hypocrites. She didn't do anything you didn't do."

The front door opened. Chaya, with her backpack, headed for the bus. The bus I should be catching, too.

"What's going on?" she asked.

"She doesn't know," Jill hissed at me. "About Ted."

"Hi!" I waved at Chaya. To her parents, I said, "And I won't tell her, if you never bring charges against Tara. If you do bring charges, I'll post this all over the world." I tossed the manila envelope.

Jill caught it. I was impressed. I'd expected the high school football player to intercept.

"Those are just copies, obviously. I have digital files." I smiled, genuinely this time, and linked my arm with Chaya's. I bent down to kiss her on the cheek, because I knew just how much it would piss off her parents.

"I need to stop home to get my bag," I said, and Chaya, looking dazed, nodded. Just to her, I added, "Come on. Tara's waiting."

Fixed it. Damn, I'm good.

VOICES CARRY

I f I didn't have such an aversion to group showers and scary women's prison wardens named Elsa, I would totally kill my parents right about now. I would beat them about the head and shoulders with my French horn.

Except I don't want to damage my French horn. Hm. Let me work on that plan.

They had to drag me to this hick town in the middle of nowhere, where in order to be in high school band, you had to be in *marching* band, too, performing at the football games everyone else cared about. That's how I ended up stomping in a prescribed pattern around the middle of a wet field of crushed grass while the trombone player behind me kept taking an extra step and nailing me right between my shoulder blades.

I don't think anyone in the metal bleachers even noticed us. (Peru Central School: Too cheap to have bleachers on both sides of the field.) Certainly they didn't make much of a noise until the short-skirted cheerleaders bounded onto the field as the band was leaving.

The school was apparently also too cheap to dry clean the

rented blue-and-white band uniforms, because mine smelled faintly of the last person to have worn it. The chin strap of the Marge-Simpson-hairdo hat dug into my chin.

Wooh. Go Indians. Rah.

I'm apparently the only person in this godforsaken school to bother to look up the fact that Peru-*really*-upstate New York is so named because the mountains in the area suggested that country to someone. Apparently that person had never *seen* the Andes, because no. Not even close. No llamas, for one thing. No brightly colored ponchos, for another.

There's very little color here in October, actually; even the famed flaming North Country leaves were muted and depressed under the lowering grey clouds. It might snow tonight. *Snow!* Jeezus.

You know what's on the Welcome to Peru website? Pictures of cows. And tractors. And old people crossing the street.

After safely stowing my French horn and hat in the band room, I returned to the game. The players, all hulked out in their gear, were trotting across the weird red track material that ran in an oval around the field to get to their starting positions. I just wanted a hot chocolate to warm me up before half-time, when we had to march again.

"Who are we playing against?" I asked Herman who, despite having lived here his whole life (and his father is one of the janitors, because name your kid "Herman" and then *kick him while he's down*), cares even less about the game than I do.

Herman plays tenor sax. He's one of those guys who'll probably be quite attractive as an adult, but right now he has to suffer through scattered acne, spindly legs, and a kind of a pointy head. We kissed once, decided it wasn't going to work, and now he's pretty much my only friend here in hell.

It's not like I'm Prom Queen material, anyway.

He squinted, his breath coming in clouded puffs, and tucked his hands in his armpits. "Beekmantown, I think."

Beekmantown, which is apparently code for Impossibly Podunk Town. As if Peru is some kind of metropolis. In both places, people shove half a bathtub upright into their front yards to make little shrines. Seriously. Kill me now.

Kill me now was my last thought before we found the body under the bleachers.

An older guy (a live one, not the dead body) was down under there, too, in the soda-cup- and napkin- and condom-littered place, looking just as shocked. He had a camera around his neck, a battered silver flask in one hand, and a reporter's notebook sticking out of the multipocketed khaki vest he wore over a thick, dark green, wool fisherman's sweater.

Without moving from where I'd stopped, I rested a hand on the icy metal strut next to me and leaned closer for a better look at the body. Him, I recognized.

Male, mid-30s, slender build, wire-rimmed glasses. Brownish hair with bits of dead brown leaves sticking in the dried blood over his right ear.

Mr. Lundy, our English teacher.

Well, that sucked.

Beside me, Herman said, "Uh...should we do something?"

"No," I said. "He's dead."

"How do you know? I mean...."

Because dead bodies aren't like you see on TV, where a live person is playing dead. Even if the actor is stellar and doesn't twitch an eyelash, no matter how much makeup you pile on 'em, they still don't look really dead.

I'd been with my grandfather when he died. He was on palliative care, finally comfortable thanks to the morphine. When they say cancer eats away at you, they aren't kidding—

that's about as apt a description there is. Grandpa was sunken, the liver spots on his head visible now that his white hair was patchy and lank. His jaw had fallen open as he drifted asleep on the good drugs, as if he didn't have the energy to close it.

My dad had taken my mom down to the hospital cafeteria for coffee. I'd listened to her complaining about the hospital cafeteria coffee as they walked away, her voice and heel-clicks fading.

So I was holding Grandpa's hand—I swear he squeezed it once or twice that afternoon, even if never opened his eyes—and reminding him of the funny family story about the enormous ceramic ALF and the burnt-orange velour sofa, and I was laughing as I told it, and then I realized he was gone.

I think he wanted to know I was happy before he could let go. I think he wanted all of us to be happy, so I hope he didn't hear my mother complaining about the goddamn coffee.

But when I say he was gone, he was *gone*. What was on the bed was an empty shell. Not asleep; not really, really still. Just no longer there.

My parents came back and my mother said "Oh God" and my father said "I'll go get someone" in a whisper (because, why? to not disturb the dead body?) and I started to tear up and my mother said, "We'll cry when we get home."

And I thought, WTF is that all about? But I didn't cry. That's not what we do.

I didn't cry at the funeral, either, because they said not to.

Then I was never able to cry later, at home or anywhere.

The hospital room had resounded with silence. The metal bleachers overhead now thrummed with people stomping their feet and cheering. Apparently our team had done something good.

The older (live) guy—maybe in his forties? I don't know. I

couldn't see any salt-and-pepper hair under his brown knit pea cap—tucked his flask into one of the many pocket in his vest and started taking pictures.

"What the hell are you doing?" I demanded.

"I'm a reporter with the *Press-Republican*," he said, as if that made it okay.

He stepped closer and I said "Don't contaminate the crime scene!" Because yeah, I do watch those stupid forensic shows, even if you know that the person they're talking to at the ten-minute mark is the killer, and you can figure out by minute forty-three why and how he dunnit.

The older guy stepped back. He dug into yet another pocket and fished out his cell phone. "I'll call 911," he said.

Above us, the crowd roared again.

"This is really going to piss everyone off," I commented. "Because I think we're winning."

THE POLICE KEPT US THERE FOREVER, ASKING QUESTIONS. I was torn between wishing I'd been able to get another hot chocolate, because I was freezing, or being glad that I hadn't, because I really had to pee.

At least I hadn't had to march in the now-cancelled half-time show. I'll take my blessings where I can find them.

As soon as they released us, I made a beeline for a Porta-Potty. I'd've rather waited until I got home, but that wasn't going to happen.

My parents stood *rightoutside*. They'd had to be there while I was questioned, and now they were sticking to me like gum on the bottom of my shoe.

Unfortunately, this meant that I could hear them.

"I wish she hadn't had to see that," my mother fretted.

I had told them I was fine, but of course they hadn't listened.

"I wonder what happened," she went on.

"Well, wasn't he one of the...you know...them?" my father said.

"Oh, right," my mother said.

Holy shit. I felt like the top of my head was going to blow off and explode the Porta-Potty. Mr. Lundy was dead and all they cared about was that he was gay? And were they assuming that's why he was dead?

I wanted to shout at them for being so ignorant, but we just didn't talk about these things. I knew they'd ignore me. So I just growled under my breath, shoved my earbuds in my ears, and played Holst's "The Planets: Jupiter" really loud all the way home.

Loud is, after all, the only way to listen to "Jupiter."

Except my hands did start shaking, once we were in the truck. Yes, we own a dark grey Ford; apparently it's the law in the North Country that you have to own a truck. Because we had to get firewood and take our own trash to the dump. The dump where, on summer evenings, I am not kidding, it's a pastime to sit and watch the black bears.

And my parents *chose* to move here.

Anyway, I started to think about Mr. Lundy, and a part of my brain thought, hm, this is what delayed shock must feel like, because I couldn't get my hands to stop shaking and "Jupiter" sounded even louder than I'd set it, and the back of my mom's headrest, with the little tear where my dad had caught it with something, seemed especially in focus.

It's not like I'd known Mr. Lundy very well or anything. He'd been my teacher. But he'd been nice, in that way some adults are nice to teenagers, treating those of us with brains like we *have* brains.

Once he'd figured out that I actually *liked* to read (and

read something other than *Twilight*. Please.), he started recommending books. *The Princess Bride* (far superior to the movie). *The Last Unicorn*. Anything by Neil Gaiman.

Mr. Lundy's chin had been a little weak, and he'd worn glasses, and had nondescript sandy brown hair, and I don't know whether he was gay or not. But I was pretty sure he didn't deserve to die.

<hr>

THE REPORTER GUY CALLED ME THE NEXT DAY. HIS NAME was Joe Dashnaw and he was normally a sports reporter, although he had co-written the front-page story. I knew all this because although my parents tried to keep it away from me, it wasn't hard to find the morning's paper in the pile next to the kindling for the woodstove in the family room.

"I can't talk to you without my parents present," I told him, which he should've remembered from yesterday.

"Off the record," he said. "I'm just curious if your memories of the incident match mine."

Well, of course you are, you bonehead. If you hadn't been drinking....

But the police hadn't said we couldn't talk to each other, and I was bored, so I said okay.

I went into the family room, where my father was dozing in the tan recliner we'd bought for Grandpa a couple of years ago, before he got really sick. A golf game was on low, and my mother was leafing through a *Better Homes and Gardens*. She and my dad had had a fight about her huge stash of them and whether we were going to truck two decades' worth of them to Peru.

I think she won, and they're in the basement somewhere. She'll never go back through them, mark my words.

I told them I was going to walk to Stewarts for some ice cream.

My mom frowned, setting the magazine next to her on the black leather sofa. "I don't want you walking anywhere alone," she said.

"Okay," I said. "Herman will go with me."

That roused my dad. He lowered the foot rest of the recliner. The springs inside twanged.

"I'm not so sure you should be spending so much time with this Herman," he said.

Oh for crying out— "He's just a *friend*," I said.

"Oh, George, it's fine," my mother said.

As if my mother would even know if we were doing it. She once said she didn't understand the purpose of premarital sex. And that, my friends, was the entirety of conversations we've had about the matter.

I was already texting Herman, and fifteen minutes later he showed up on my doorstep, and off we went.

It's probably stupid to out for ice cream in October, but it felt warmer today because the sun was actually out, and ice cream is ice cream after all.

Stewart's Shops were unique to upstate New York. The chain sold gas and some basic groceries; there was some sort of Milk Club where if you bought ten cartons of milk, you got a free one. They still used index cards to keep track.

They also sold their own ice cream, in gallons or in cones or cups. Each shop had a couple of Formica tables. Mr. Dashnaw was sitting at one, and raised a hand when we entered.

I ordered Adirondack Bear Paw (vanilla, caramel, and cashew crunch) in a cup, because someday I'll escape this godforsaken place and I won't be able to have this ever again. Herman hesitated, and I knew it was because he didn't have the money. So I ordered him a Black Raspberry and told him he owed me one.

We slid onto the curved, hard orange bench across from Mr. Dashnaw. He had a cup of coffee cradled between his hands. He looked better today that he had yesterday. His eyes were brighter, somehow, and he just seemed less…rumpled.

"Do the police have any leads?" I asked, and realized I sounded like a bad cliché.

Mr. Dashnaw shook his head. "Not really. Autopsy said he was hit on the back of the head. You know, they say most people are killed by someone they know."

What did that mean? His partner? A closet gay-basher?

My hands started to shake again, and I stuffed them between my thighs, as if I were trying to warm them.

"I didn't see any footprints," Herman commented around a mouthful of ice cream.

The ground under the bleachers was patchy dead grass, hard-packed mud, and scattered trash. But I remembered when we walked under there that I'd been kicking at the clumps of grass, upturning them, and there had been other areas of fresher mud.

"I don't think he would've just been hanging out under there," I said. "Maybe he was dragged there."

"Didn't he jog on the track after school?" Herman asked. I turned and stared at him.

He shrugged. "Sometimes I stay late and my dad drives me home when he's done work."

Come to think of it, he *had* been wearing sweatpants and a hoodie and sneakers. That hadn't even occurred to me until now.

Mr. Dashnaw asked if we knew about Mr. Lundy's home life, which we didn't. We talked a little more and then he said, "Thanks, kids. This might be the break I need. I'm really sick of sports reporting."

And I thought, awesome. Someone's dead and it's a way to further your career? But of course I didn't say it aloud, except to Herman, on the way home.

When I got home, my mother said, "Mrs. Fessette said she saw you at Stewart's talking to that reporter."

Crap. I *suck* at lying. I always end up with a big goofy grin on my face. "Yeah, he was there," I said. Truth. "He's really a sports reporter." Also truth.

I thought about Mr. Lundy, dead, and I didn't smile.

"I just don't want him upsetting you," my mother said.

"I'm fine," I said. Okay, that was a lie. But it was the kind we told each other all the time.

I couldn't fall asleep that night, no matter what type of music I listened to: baroque, rock, country. Tears clung to the back of my throat, scraped the backs of my eyes. Maybe if I slammed my hand in a door, I'd be able to cry.

No, then I wouldn't be able to play French horn. Have to work on that plan, too.

Tuesday night was the viewing, at the Brown Funeral Home in Plattsburgh. The main part of it had been an old house, and they'd tacked an extra part on, or maybe extended to meet up with the carriage house, hard to tell. It was painted white, with a zig-zag stone-edged walkway for people who couldn't get up the stairs.

I guess a lot of old people go to funerals. Now there's a depressing thought.

Inside was slate-blue acanthus-leaf wallpaper and gilt-framed paintings and dark wood furniture. It smelled overwhelmingly of flowers, all the different scents jumbled up and cloying.

Mr. Lundy's partner wore a new-looking dark suit, but the toes of his loafers were scuffed, and his hair was messy. I realized I recognized him: he owned the only used bookstore in Plattsburgh, a tiny place jammed full of books, with a rickety staircase that I was always sure was going to come crashing down under my weight and that of the volumes stacked along the edges.

We shuffled through the line. I looked at Mr. Lundy in the coffin. He looked worse then when we'd found the body, I thought. Now he looked waxy, fake.

We got to Mr. Lundy's partner, and I realized I didn't know his name. His eyes were red around the edges, but he managed a smile when I told him Mr. Lundy had been my teacher and I would miss him. I wanted to tell him about the books he'd recommended, but I couldn't. It was like I was suddenly, stupidly shy. But I couldn't get the words out; they stuck with the tears in my throat.

My father shook his hand, his voice hearty, as it always was when he was uncomfortable. My mother simply descended into unflinchingly polite mode, overemphasizing to convey fake emotion.

I wanted to kick them in the shins.

My mouth was dry, so I took a bottle of water and stood off to the side with Herman, who'd ridden with us. His hair was slicked over and he looked uncomfortable in his dress pants, which were a little short, and white shirt.

I tried to drink, but had trouble swallowing.

The reception line dwindled, and Mr. Lundy's partner sat down in a corner with people he obviously knew well. I wanted to leave, but my parents were talking to the Fessettes, and when my mother gets talking, God help us. Eventually my father would get bored and start poking her in the waist with a finger to get her moving.

Mr. Lundy's partner covered his face with his hands, and I saw his shoulders shaking.

Something hurt, deep and sharp in my stomach. Not exactly like wanting to throw up, not like appendicitis. More like something cracking, breaking.

And that's when I cried. Not for me, because I hadn't known Mr. Lundy all that well, but for his partner. For his parents. For the people who loved him, because he was gone and they would never have him again.

Then I realized I was lying to myself. I was crying for them, but I was also crying for me—for Grandpa.

My mother hurried over and put her arm around me. "No, no," she said. "You're not supposed to be sad."

Which was a stupid thing to say, and it only made me cry harder. She started digging in her voluminous purse for a Kleenex, but I knew all about her scary, crumpled, holey Kleenexes, and I squirmed out of her grasp and reached around for the handy box nearby. Funeral homes clearly buy them in bulk at Sam's Club, and for good reason.

My father said, "Maybe it's time to go," and I said, "I have to go to the bathroom," and that made them happy because at least I wouldn't be making a public scene anymore.

Nobody spoke on the drive back to Peru, through the dark and the cold. Herman patted my hand, and I suddenly gripped his, glad for his touch.

No, not that way.

The police figured out that Mr. Lundy had been killed by a transient, a drug addict who'd approached him for money. The guy had been living in the woods on the other side of all the sports fields, and that's where they found him.

The fact that he'd been so close to the school was some scary shit. I half-thought my parents were going to decide Peru wasn't any safer than anywhere else we'd lived, but we'd moved here for my father's job, and the guy had been passing through, apparently. Headed south, where it's not so freaking cold.

My parents don't say anything about me losing it at the funeral home. They're probably not going to like it when the essay I wrote about Mr. Lundy gets published in the *Press-Republican*, because I mention his partner. They're not going to like the fact that I've realized that I maybe have a crush on a girl.

But you know what? I can talk about it with somebody else.

Because life is too short not to cry and not to say what's in your heart.

CLAP YOUR HANDS IF YOU BELIEVE

I sat in my car and looked at the high, grey walls of the prison, made all the more oppressive by the equally grey clouds lining the sky and the dirty snow pressed against the base of the fortress-like building and clumped in patches around the parking lot where a snowplow had shoved it weeks before. Winter in the North Country: dismal, depressing, and seemingly never-ending.

I could sympathize with people who suffered from SAD.

Already the cold seeped into my car, mere minutes after I'd turned it off. It wasn't the subfreezing temperature that made me loathe to leave the car.

No, it was the simple fact that I'd rather be anywhere but here, doing anything but this.

In all honesty, it made sense that Bob, my editor, had sent me to do the interview. Jennifer Duschanes responded better to women, although she hadn't yet told anyone why she'd done what she'd done. She'd pleaded not guilty, the jury had thought otherwise, and she'd been sentenced to life in prison.

Psychological reports indicated dissociative disorder of

some sort. Family and friends insisted she'd shown no signs of mental illness of any kind, nor did her health records.

"She'd seemed a little distracted," her husband, Paul, had said in a rare interview. "But we both were, getting ready for Christmas." His voice broke when he added, "She loved making a big deal out of Christmas for the kids."

And so here I was, having been dispatched to interview Jennifer Duschanes on the one-year anniversary of her Christmas Eve poisoning her children.

***

It was chilly in the visiting room, too. I'd had to leave my wool coat at the entrance, but at least I had my scarf wound around my neck. I wrapped my hands in the ends to warm them.

The fluorescent lighting was harsh; the cinderblock walls—painted a shade of off-white that had probably been on discount—metal table and chairs, and pale green linoleum floor were doctor's-office pristine but held no warmth.

My digital recorder was on the table. I didn't bother taking the file out of my messenger bag; I knew the details, even though I didn't want to. Even though I'd done everything I could to forget them, until Bob had thrust this assignment on me.

Jennifer Duschanes had been a smart, attractive, upper-middle-class wife and mother. She ran a successful home business selling essential oils. Her own upbringing had been normal: two parents, happy home. She and Paul had a marriage that he, even after the fact, insisted had been wonderful. They'd adored their children, and she loved working from home so she had more time with them. The children had also shown no signs of anything being wrong at home; they got good grades, were praised for good behavior, got along well with their peers.

When arrested, she'd been calm, insisting she'd been taking care of the children, that everything was fine. She never publicly explained why.

The door opened, and I stood, surprised at a rush of relief. I hadn't been locked in, but just now I realized I'd felt that way, trapped.

A thin female deputy escorted Jennifer in. Apparently Jennifer wasn't considered a threat, because she wore no handcuffs.

I'd seen pictures of her, and discovered now that she was as classically pretty as those photos had depicted. She was a natural blond—no roots—and despite her lack of makeup, her skin was smooth. Good bones, my mother would have said. Good genes.

"Hello," I said, sitting back down as she slipped into the metal chair across the table from me. The guard caught my eye, and I nodded. I honestly didn't feel afraid; I knew the guard would be right outside the door, and Jennifer Duschanes had never shown even an inkling of violence.

I wasn't afraid, but I didn't want to be here, not with her.

"Hi," she said. "Esme Blaylock, right? From the *County Star*?"

"That's right," I said.

"You look tired," she said. She cocked her head. "New-mother tired."

It was a sixth sense that new mothers shared: We could tell when another woman was in the same state of exhaustion/elation. Not a pregnancy glow, but a recently-given-birth pallor.

I didn't want to tell her, didn't want to give her an edge, but despite that I heard myself say, "She's teething."

"Oh, that's a rough time," she said, understanding in her

blue eyes, and she leaned towards me, her hand in mid-air before she paused and pulled herself back, obviously remembering the No Touching rule of prison visitation.

A model prisoner.

I clamped down on the rest of it: that my husband was deployed; that I wasn't from the area and missed family and friends; that living off-base, working full-time, and having a newborn meant I hadn't connected with the usual social group. That until this interview, the newspaper had made a point of assigning me stories close to home, and often let me do the write-up and file the story from home. That I wasn't used to the cold, the grey, the unending nights.

That last night my husband had confirmed that no, he wasn't able to get leave to be home for what should have been our first Christmas as a family.

Jennifer smiled. It wasn't the smile of a cold-blooded killer, a psychopath with no concept of remorse or consequences. It was…sort of wistful. "You understand, then," she said. "What it's like to a mother in this world." The smile faded; she turned inward, her eyes no longer seeing me. "They grow up so fast, don't they?"

Hers wouldn't. Not Mabel, called Mae, named for her grandmother; not little Andy, the tow-headed charmer of his preschool. They were frozen in time at seven and four years old.

I didn't say that, either, of course. If I antagonized Jennifer, accused her, she wouldn't talk to me.

I had a job to do, and I needed to do it and get out of here. Get home and check on Layla; write up the story and file it for tomorrow's edition; and review my schedule for tomorrow and the next day.

Christmas Eve and Christmas Day. If Jake wasn't going to be home, and Layla was too young to understand the holiday,

I figured I might as well volunteer to cover the shifts so other reporters could be home with their families.

Both days would be light, news-wise. I'd call the cops, get the scoop on homes that had caught on fire thanks to a sparking woodstove or a frayed Christmas-light cord, on who drove drunk home from a party. I'd write a fluff piece about day-after-Christmas sales. One of the print room guys would slip me a cup of eggnog spiked with naughty rum, which I wouldn't drink because all I cared about was finishing my shift and getting home to my baby.

I reached for the digital recorder on the metal table between us, thumbed it on. "You're fine with me recording this?"

She leaned in slightly. "Of course, yes, no problem."

I had pad and pen as well, although my fingers were stiff from the chill. "Thank you, I appreciate your taking the time to talk to me."

Her pretty mouth twisted in a wry grin. "I've got nowhere else to be."

I'd rehearsed this on the way up, but hadn't found an opening question that didn't make my skin crawl. "It's been a year since...the tragedy. Do you have any new perspective on what happened?" I shied away from *what you did* and *why, for the love of God, you monster*.

I didn't want to know. As a reporter, I reluctantly supposed I did, but as a mother, as a human being...

She looked thoughtful, considering my question. "New perspective," she repeated. "No, I don't think so. I..." She stopped, looked directly at me. "You want to know why I did it, don't you?"

Yes. No.

She slowly nodded. "You have a baby. You know what it's like. I think...I think you'll understand."

My breath caught, and I tried not to show any of the

conflicting emotions I felt. On one hand, it sounded as though she was going to give me the scoop of my small career. On the other hand, I wanted to plug my ears and close my eyes, the same as I did during autopsy scenes on crime shows.

"Please," I said. "Take your time."

Her blue eyes took on a distant cast as she obviously relived the memory. And then, for the first time, Jennifer Duschanes told her story.

SHE'D READ AN ARTICLE A FEW YEARS AGO, SHE SAID, ABOUT homeless children in Miami who'd created their own mythology, of a Blue Lady who protected them. The story haunted her long after she read it. She could imagine the children, filthy and hungry, huddled together to tell tales that would make them feel safe, maybe even loved.

But isn't that what fairy tales are for? Like religion, they instruct, and bring us comfort through their archetypes.

There's magic all around us, if you keep the faith.

When she read that article, she thought of her own children: well-fed, warmly dressed, safe and loved.

They didn't need magic the way the children in Miami did. But everyone needs enchantment. The world would be such a grey place without it.

She'd mostly forgotten about that article until the day Mae came home from first grade. She heard the front door open, and the rumble of the departing schoolbus. Mae came into the kitchen, cheeks rosy from the winter air, angelic blond hair touseling free of the sparkly pink plastic clip.

Mae hugged her mother's waist and then opened the fridge. "There's no Santa Claus."

Not a question—a statement. Jennifer set down the baking sheet of sugar cookies and struggled to find a reply.

"Why do you say that, honey?" A question would buy her a little time.

Mae selected an apple. She'd lost her top two front teeth recently, but she loved apples, and was content to gnaw semi-successfully at them, leaving a red, uneaten trail down the middle.

"Because it's true. Besides..." She cocked her head, in an almost-adult gesture that broke Jennifer's heart further. "You use the same wrapping paper."

Damn. It had never occurred to her to have "Santa" use a signature pattern.

Jennifer didn't even have to confirm or deny. Mae knew the truth, and was simply sharing her newfound knowledge. Mae awkwardly crunched into the apple and wandered off. Jennifer leaned against the counter. Water, splashed from the sink, seeped into her jeans, but she didn't care. Her hands trembled, and she put the dish towel down.

Mae was growing up. They'd have to ask her not to tell her brother the news about Santa. Andy was only four; he wasn't ready to have his dreams shattered.

That's what it was all about, wasn't it? Broken dreams? Lies your parents told you—magic you clung to until the cold harsh reality of the world beat you down. Believing was for babies, or fools, or crazy people.

Believing was not for responsible adults.

She turned and plunged her hands into the dishwater, now lukewarm and barely sudsy, but she didn't pick up the plate beneath her fingers.

This past summer—just a few short months ago—they'd been on the ferry to Burlington and Mae had cried out, pointing to the water fairies. They were just sparkles of light on the choppy water, sunlight catching on the wavelets.

No. They were water fairies.

Jennifer saw them, too.

A few weeks after that, a friend of theirs went to a rock concert, and at the end the band shot confetti over the audience. When the fine bits of tissue paper caught in the light, they twisted and glittered and shone. The friend, having heard the water fairies tale, told Mae that she'd seen concert fairies, and Mae had been in awe.

Jennifer believed in the concert fairies. Mae, no doubt, would soon discount that story, too.

What was next? she wondered. Would Mae put away her Barbies, pull down her unicorn posters, and scoff at Disney?

Jennifer tried to imagine Mae and Andy living in a bleak world without magic, and she despaired.

A mother's strongest instinct is to protect her children.

"So that became my goal…you might call it an obsession," Jennifer said. "To protect them, to make sure they didn't lose the magic. Like in *Peter Pan*, you know? Keeping Tinkerbell alive by believing in her, by clapping your hands if you believe."

Protecting one's children and murdering them were two different things in my book, but I tucked my cold fingers in my scarf and nodded. "I remember that in *Peter Pan*," I said.

I remembered seeing a stage production with my parents, and clapping my little hands so hard they stung. Because I *believed*.

That didn't mean I understood now.

Jennifer continued, although there wasn't much left for her to say. She did everything she could to make that Christmas extra-magical, even spending time online looking for more ideas, crafts, and surprises to dazzle Mae and Andy.

On Christmas Eve, she convinced her husband to go outside

and brush a little snow off the roof so it would fall by the window of the bedroom the children shared that night, quivering in anticipation of Santa's imminent arrival. Even Mae was swept up in the excitement, and it made Jennifer's heart sing.

She gave the children some warm milk and honey to help them sleep, then tucked them in, and as their eyelids finally began to droop, she texted her husband to ring faint jingle bells outside the window.

The children squealed in delight, then drifted off after she promised them the only way Santa would come down the chimney once they were fast asleep.

Mae and Andy didn't wake up the next morning. The hallucinogenic mushroom she'd crumbled into their milk had killed them.

In her quest to make Christmas magical, Jennifer Duschanes had stumbled across an article discussing how shamans in Lapland ingested a certain type of mushroom that made them believe the saw reindeers fly, a legend that became part of the traditional Santa Claus stories.

Although she didn't say it in so many words, I understood that Jennifer hadn't mean to kill her children. She'd thought the hallucinogens would help them see what they wanted to see, believe in the enchantment of Christmas and the existence of water fairies and the Easter Bunny and Disney heroes.

But her final words were what stuck with me, would always echo in me.

Or maybe it was the contented smile on her face as she hugged herself and spoke with utter belief.

"So you see, Esme, everything is fine. Nothing can hurt them now. They'll never stop believing in the fairy tales they so desperately need, and they'll never, ever be without magic. I protected them. They're safe."

<hr>

My boots crunched in the frozen slush as I slogged across the parking lot, and my breath puffed out, another shade of grey in this harsh grey world.

I threw my bag in the passenger seat, started the car, willed the heated seat to thaw the deep chill inside me. No, not so much chill as just being numb.

Eventually I just started driving to the home that didn't feel like home, through a world that didn't feel like Christmastime, even though new flakes were drifting down and I had to drive more carefully in the deepening gloom.

I didn't want to report crime. I didn't want to be reminded, time and again, of the horrors of the world. I wanted to hold my baby and protect her from knowing those horrors.

When I finally arrived home, I paid the babysitter and made sure she drove away safely. I had a story to write and file.

Not yet. Give me a few minutes.

In the doorway to Layla's bedroom, I watched her sleeping, soft and innocent, and I felt the thaw start, hard and painful in my core, spreading out. I went in and lifted her out of the crib, blankets and all, and cradled her against my chest. She felt warm, and as I nuzzled her, I inhaled her familiar, special milky-sweet scent.

"Don't worry," I whispered, my lips against her fine hair. "I'll keep you safe. I won't let you get hurt by the bad things or the sad things in the world.

"I'll make sure you always believe in fairies."

WOMEN WHO LOVE DOGS

There is nothing better than being greeted by a dog that loves you. They wriggle from shoulder to tail and back again, as if their joy, their adoration for you can't be contained, as if the uncontrollable motion keeps them from bursting apart in a flurry of fur and pure, trusting devotion.

Vanessa Sheridan buried her face in Merlin's fur, not caring about the doggy smell or the slight oiliness in his soft fur. Her whole world shrank down to this touch, this moment. He stilled a little, as if realizing she needed to hide her tear-stained face in him, and leaned his solid body gently against her crouched form.

"You heard?"

Brooke's voice held the nasally muffle of someone who'd been crying.

Vanessa sighed, letting a tiny bit of the tension of out of her shoulders, then stood and closed the door of the small bottom-floor apartment she shared with her sister, a year and half younger than her. Closed it against the sheeting rain that had made her midnight-drive home from the newspaper a white-knuckled one, closed it against the evils of the world as best she could.

"I did," she said.

Brooke had turned on every lamp in the room probably for the same reason. The brightness was almost too much, adding to the headache vibrating out of Vanessa's tight neck muscles. It drove away the shadows but didn't hide the flaws.

The clumps of dog fur at the corners of the scuffed hardwood floors, persistent no matter how often Vanessa vacuumed. The barely better than college furniture, mismatched but comfortable: a dark blue oversized easy chair; a blue, burgundy, and green sofa in a pattern best described as "dated"; an antique oak coffee table that Vanessa had refinished in high school, which had taught her she hated refinishing furniture and would never do it again.

The rolling walker with the small black seat, crouched next to one end of the sofa like a four-legged metal spider.

Vanessa sat next to Brooke on the sofa, and Merlin jumped up and laid down on the other side, resting his head on Brooke's skinny thigh. He wasn't an official service dog—the MS hadn't progressed so far that Brooke needed constant care —but he'd had some training, and he was smart and devoted.

"It's all over Twitter, and it was on the eleven o'clock news," Brooke said, grabbing Vanessa's hand. Brooke's skin was cold, dry.

Vanessa had known for several hours—working at a newspaper meant you heard news as fast as it hit social media.

The latest victim in a string of rapes up and down the Southern California coast had been identified as their friend Camila Hernandez.

Camila had been their classmate at Ventura College—same year as Vanessa, both of them two years ahead of Brooke—and had gone on to study veterinary science. She was Merlin's vet, in fact. Vanessa clenched her fists again, an action she'd been doing the whole drive home, wishing she could have somehow been there, somehow have helped.

"We'll call tomorrow and see if she's up for visitors," Vanessa said. "I'll have time before work." As the copy editor, she worked the late shift at the local paper, 2 to 10 p.m.—or later, like tonight, when there was last-minute news to include in the morning edition.

"Sounds good." Brooke managed a trembly smile.

Brooke didn't need this kind of stress. Vanessa gathered her into a hug. She'd promised her parents she'd take care of her sister. Promised herself. No matter how hard she tried, she couldn't protect Brooke from this.

When Vanessa got up from the sofa a few moments later, Merlin raised his head, tail thumping expectantly.

"Yes, it's time for your walk," Vanessa said. She was exhausted emotionally and mentally, and her warm, dry bed sang a seductive siren call, a counterpoint to the constant waterfall of rain. But when you had a dog, you had to walk it. The rare rain made it more of a burden than its normal pleasure.

They'd had to find an affordable apartment that was on the ground floor and handicapped accessible, not on a hill (which was along one side of Ventura, California) for Brooke's needs, not too close to the beach (on the other side) because those were too expensive, and with a yard for Merlin. One too many requirements; something had to give, and that was the yard. They had a tiny cement patio ringed with an edging of small rocks and a few scattered succulents, and at worst, Merlin could pee there in an emergency.

"He had a playdate today, so he shouldn't need much more than a potty break," Brooke said.

"Small blessings," Vanessa said. She dug an umbrella out of

the tiny front closet, grabbed Merlin's leash from the hook by the door. Once more unto the breach.

"Be safe," Brooke called as Vanessa went out.

The rain was cold, and the air had a strange cast to it—when you lived in the desert by the ocean, anything more humid than *arid* was unusual. Streetlights wavered, pressing against the darkness, obscured by the sheets of rain.

Still, Vanessa didn't feel afraid. She had Merlin, for one thing. For another, in each of the eleven cases, the rapist—or maybe a group of guys trading off—was the one with the dog. Every victim had spoken, at some point in the preceding days, to a man walking a dog.

The problem: each victim described a different man, and each victim remembered a different kind of dog.

Witnesses rarely got all their facts straight. Everyone knew that. Ask ten people who just saw a car accident what what kind of car and what color, and you were going to get answers ranging from a two-door to a sedan to an SUV, and from red to blue to black.

The victims agreed that the man was of slender-to-medium build, and average height. They disagreed on hair color and style, eye color, and facial hair. They agreed that the dogs were on the larger side and friendly. They disagreed on breed (although several had said "mutt" or indefinable), color, and fur.

Now, like a typical dog, Merlin trotted over to a fire hydrant and relieved himself, unconcerned with the rain. She'd have to dry him off when they got back, *before* he got the chance to shake himself.

It felt better to think about mundane things: drying off the dog, grabbing a quick shower, making a quick shopping list for the Farmer's Market tomorrow. Better than thoughts of work, and men who attacked women, and Camila.

HE'S WALKING ON THE BEACH, MID-AFTERNOON. HE'S calling himself John this time. A bland, common name: easy to remember, easy to forget. The sand is damp and dark and packed from the rain, which finally eased up a couple of hours ago. Everything smells of brine and fish because of the random clumps of slimy strands that have washed up. Clouds still scud across the sky, but there are patches where the sun can get through, golden light streaking down to kiss the ocean beyond the pier.

When the clouds move across the sun, they glow, as if God is watching.

He lets the dog off the leash. It runs at the low waves, barking, then races back. John finds a stick and hurls it, and the dog, true to its breed, chases, grabs the stick in its jaws, returns.

He throws the stick again, this time in a direction such that the dog's run will intersect the path of a female jogger. Distracted, the dog abandons the stick to greet a new potential friend. The woman stops and ruffles the dog's fur. The dog dances around her slender runner's legs.

John moves while she's distracted, making it look as though he's just walking down the beach, which brings him in range of her, casually.

She looks up. Her caramel-streaked hair is in a ponytail, but wisps have escaped, fluttering in the ocean breeze. Her cheeks are pink and her eyes are bright from her run.

"Hi," she says with a breathless smile, both from the exercise and, he can tell, from petting the dog. "Is he yours?"

"He is," he says. "I call him Chowder."

It's not the dog's name; he's forgotten the dog's name, actually. No matter. *Chowder* is adorable, especially for a dog on or in a seaside park. They all say so.

"What an adorable name," the woman says.

He has a list of equally adorable names that he swaps out regularly.

"Thanks," he says. He keeps his hands in his windbreaker pockets, his shoulders relaxed. Casual. Unthreatening. Today his wig is dark blond, in a rumpled, could-be-a-surfer style, and his contacts are blue, and he's let just enough five-o'clock shadow show.

"Hey, are you a dog person?" he asks. "I'm new to the area and looking for a good vet."

This one is a dog person; she has two Papillions at home. She tells him about her vet, and he asks all the right questions that draw out of her the area she lives in (by asking housing questions, since he's still looking), and where she works (she goes to Ventura College during the day and tends bar at Cassidy's on Santa Clara downtown most evenings—he should drop by during happy hour; they have half-priced well drinks and appetizers).

She doesn't realize how much she reveals in a few short moments of conversation. He's a dog person, trustworthy.

And she had approached him. She had said hello first. She had shown interest. That was the important thing: she approached him.

"Well, I've gotta go," she says. "Bye, Chowder. Bye, Chowder's dad."

She takes off down the beach. He's careful not to watch her. He throws the stick for the dog again. He really is a dog person; that's how he found out how much women loved dogs, how women found men with dogs approachable.

He is startled, thrown off, when he hear her voice close by. They never turn around, not at this point.

It excites him in a way he'd never felt before.

"Hi, sorry," she says breathlessly. "I think my ring fell off when I was petting Chowder. Do you see it anywhere?"

Chowder unhelpfully runs around their feet as they look until the man tells him to sit, which he obediently does, mouth open and smiling, panting up at them as they kick through the sand.

"Well, damn," she says finally. "It was my class ring. That's what I get for wearing it when I'm working out. Thanks for trying."

She takes off again.

John sees it as an amazing sign. She approached him *twice*. Surely she won't reject him later.

Not like the others, inexplicably, did.

"SOMETHING'S WRONG WITH MERLIN," BROOKE SAID WHEN Vanessa got home from her dentist appointment.

"I wondered," Vanessa said. "He was kind of listless on his walk this morning."

"He threw up—and it didn't look like he'd been eating grass," Brooke said. She looked as though she was struggling not to cry.

Vanessa knew the last few days had been hard on her. Visiting Camila had been draining: their friend had tried to smile, tried to welcome them into her parents' home where she was staying for awhile, but every time Vanessa and Brooke stopped talking, Camila...faded away. Lost herself in the bad memories.

Plus Brooke's MS symptoms were flaring up thanks to the heat. The rain was gone, and even though Ventura normally stayed twenty degrees cooler than the Valley and LA, the Santa Anas were now blowing, the scorching, arid winds that came over the desert to the east, sucking the moisture out of everything, making you feel as if you were being mummified from the inside out.

Brooke didn't need added stress.

They took Merlin to the local emergency vet, where Merlin even managed a few wags of his tail at the white-coated tech who took him back to be x-rayed.

"Good news," the vet said a little while later, shoving the processed x-rays into the clip at the top of the display lamp. He was a small, bald man, although he looked strong enough to heave a Newfoundland onto the examining table if he needed to. Behind his wire-rimmed glasses, his blue eyes were kind.

"See this here?" he asked, pointing with a ballpoint pen bearing the clinic's logo. "Looks like ol' Merlin swallowed a magic ring. It's small enough to pass through him normally; he'll be back to himself in about two days. He might throw up again once or twice—that's normal—but if he's in any greater distress, bring him back in."

THE EMERGENCY VET VISIT WASN'T CHEAP, BUT THANKFULLY it didn't break the bank, either. Brooke did accounting for a number of different nonprofits in town (allowing her to work at home) and Vanessa's editing job was solid. They'd be fine.

And right on schedule, Merlin passed the ring.

"Yippie," Vanessa muttered as she wrapped her hand in a doggie disposal bag and picked the glinting silver out of the soft poop, breathing through her mouth so she didn't have to smell it. She shoved the plastic wrapped ring in the pocket of her jean shorts and picked up the rest of the poop to toss.

Merlin sat and grinned at her, tongue hanging out, tail thumping against the grass.

"Well, I'm glad you're feeling better," she told him. She flung the tennis ball she'd brought along, and he bounded after it.

They were at one of the seaside parks, a big grassy area ringed by a concrete jogging/bike path. Little kids with helmets firmly buckled on their heads pedaled their tricycles with grim concentration. On the other side of the path, past the sandy volleyball area, ice-plant covered dunes rose toward the clear blue sky. They blocked the view of the ocean, but not the smell of wet and salt.

Over by the covered picnic tables, a trim blond personal trainer was putting three students through their workout, having them step up on the concrete benches, do a squat, step down, do a squat, and then do it all over again. Vanessa's quads burned in sympathy.

Keeping one eye on Merlin, Vanessa turned on a tap outside the stone bathrooms. It was low down, designed to let people wash the sand off their feet before they headed to their cars, but she always found it useful for filling Merlin's travel bowl. Now, though, she stuck the poop-covered ring under the stream until the piece of jewelry was no longer poop-covered, then she wiped it approximately eight million times with paper towels.

She'd assumed it would be one of hers or Brooke's. She was wrong.

It was a class ring from Santa Clarita High Schools. When Vanessa saw the inscription, she felt a wash of cold run through her, and despite the heat, she shivered. Bile washed up into her throat.

The name had been released to the media last night.

Jessamyn Dupree. Twenty-two. College student, bartender.

Latest rape victim.

JOHN IS ASTOUNDED AND FURIOUS. WHY HAD JESSAMYN rejected him? She'd approached him twice. *Twice.* That showed clear interest in him. An obvious desire for him.

But in the end she'd turned out to be just another cock-tease, another fake. He'd waited for her after her shift at the bar, offered—like a gentleman—to walk her home, but then she'd tried to surreptitiously dial 911 on her phone.

Normally he leaves town after his ordeals. Rents another dog, tries again. But he's been rattled by this one. He's angry —no, he's furious. He doesn't want to wait this time.

He wants to try again to find the woman who will accept him, who won't turn away from him.

OFFICER ORTIZ LED THEM IN TO A SMALL ROOM, WITH JUST benches on either side. The gunmetal grey doorway was narrow, and it took a moment for Brooke to maneuver her walker through. He looked uncomfortable, as if he were making a mental note that the problem needed to be fixed.

Vanessa made sure Brooke was settled on the wooden bench before she sat next to her. It was hard and uncomfort-able, and the room smelled of cheap air freshener and the body odor the spray was supposed to have covered up. Officer Ortiz sat across from them. His uniform looked a little too big, as if he'd lost weight recently, although he looked fine for his lanky, tall frame. His dark mustache was trim, his hair buzzed.

He held Jessamyn Dupree's ring in a clear plastic evidence bag.

"Where do you think your dog was when he ate the ring?" he asked.

"I walk him twice a day," Vanessa said, "but I keep a close

eye on him, so I think think it happened near our apartment."

"But he's also signed up for Rent-a-Pup," Brooke said.

Officer Ortiz raised his eyebrows.

"It's an online service that basically rents dogs to other people," Brooke explained. She was looking a little better, a little stronger in the air conditioned station. "Because golden retrievers need to get out and run, and it's hard for us to give Merlin that, we signed up for it. We pay an annual fee, and people who want to rent dogs do, too."

Ortiz shook his head. "I'm not sure I get it."

"There are people who love dogs but can't have one for some reason," Vanessa said. "Maybe they're in an apartment that doesn't allow pets, or someone in the house is allergic, or they work really long hours. It's their chance to spend time with a dog."

Ortiz might not have been up on the latest sharing economy schemes, but he wasn't stupid, either. "So you think the person who rented your dog raped Jessamyn Dupree?"

"His name is John Flynn," Brooke said, fishing a printout from her purse and handing it to him. "Here's the application he filled out. When he came to pick up and drop off Merlin, he had blond, shaggy hair like a surfer, and blue eyes. I don't remember anything else specific about him, though." She hunched her shoulders. "He seemed nice," she added, her voice thin.

Officer Ortiz took the paper. "If he paid with a credit card, we may be able to trace it." He stood, held out his hand. "Thank you, ladies. Because of you, we may just be able to nail this sonuvabitch. I'll call you if we have any follow-up questions."

It was Vanessa who called the police station again the very next morning, asking for Officer Ortiz. Doing everything she could to keep her voice from shaking, she told him that through the Rent-a-Pup website, they'd received another request from John Flynn to rent Merlin again that day.

***

John knows something is wrong as he approaches the apartment. Something is off, something is tense. Too quiet, somehow.

The anger grows inside him like the rising tide at the full moon. What has the skinny girl with the walker done? Has she rejected him, too? He didn't want her, not in that way, but still...

He likes her dog. He didn't think someone with such a nice dog could be such a betraying bitch.

He knows he should turn, walk away, but it may be too late. Then he'll have to spend so much time explaining why, explaining how it's *their* fault, how he's only punishing them for accepting and then rejecting him, for leading him along.

And his rage for the skinny walker girl is a red wash across his vision, like when you lie on a hot beach with your eyes closed and the sun tries to pierce your lids.

He practices his easy smile. Drops his shoulders. Tucks his hands casually in his jeans pocket.

Wraps his fingers around the knife.

***

Vanessa understood what Merlin must have felt after he'd eaten the ring. She wanted nothing more than to throw up, then curl into a little ball with Merlin, just like she'd done when she was a kid and was sad and so she snuggled with their beagle, Sparky.

There had been no time to set up an undercover officer, no time to figure anything else out. If they delayed in telling John he could rent Merlin, they ran the risk of losing him.

So she stood in the living room with the mismatched furniture and dog fur in the corners of the wooden floor and waited for the doorbell to ring.

When she answered it, the police would arrest him.

Brooke was around the corner, in an unmarked car, with Officer Ortiz. Safe. That was all Vanessa cared about. That and stopping the rapist from ever hurting another woman again.

The bell rang, and she nearly screamed, and understood the concept of nearly jumping out of one's skin. She could smell her own acrid sweat, knew her shirt was damp under her arms. Merlin sat on the sofa where she'd told him to stay.

Her hand was shaking so hard, she almost couldn't flip the deadbolt or twist the knob.

He moved inside so quickly that she couldn't react other than to step back, step away from his closeness. He was, as reported, of average build, and she wasn't a small woman, but his presence was overpowering.

The blank look in his eyes. Which were brown. His natural color? Or contacts? It was a stupid thing to wonder, and anyway, her world was focusing down to the knife in his hand.

"Where's the skinny bitch?" he asked, eyes flicking past her. "The one with the walker?"

Vanessa opened her mouth to answer but didn't know what to say. Dimly she heard someone shout "Police! Freeze!" and the man—John—the rapist grabbed her arm and pulled her hard against him, and then Merlin made a noise she'd never heard before.

She knew the growl he made when he saw a ground squirrel or gopher.

This growl was nothing like that. This was terrifying—and yet somehow comforting.

Merlin launched himself from the sofa and over the coffee table in a leap she'd never imagined he could do. John shouted and held out the knife, but Merlin landed and sank his teeth into the man's leg. John yelled in pain and let go of Vanessa, and as she fell to the side, she saw the knife come down, and then she heard a very, very loud bang that reverberated and rang in her ears even after it was over.

John loves dogs, and he doesn't understand why the dog attacked him. John had only been trying to protect himself.

Unlike women, dogs never reject him.

Until now.

His leg throbs in time with his heart.

Vanessa pressed her face into Merlin's soft, stinky fur. The man hadn't stabbed Merlin, not in the end. He'd dropped the knife as the police shot, as near as anyone could tell.

Nobody else had been hurt. Everyone was safe.

Brooke was safe.

She was shaking again, this time from the aftermath of adrenaline and fear and shock. But holding on to Merlin kept her from bursting apart.

PIRATE PETE'S

There weren't many places for teenagers to find summer employment in the Florida Heartland in the summer of 1983, and even fewer places for teenagers to hang out. The ocean was too far. The lake worked in a pinch for some, if they were close enough, but it tended to be overrun with families and fishermen. There were no malls yet, not even in Sebring.

But there was Pirate Pete's Adventureland.

Built several decades before as a kiddie amusement park —which is still was on summer days—it became a gathering place for bored teens at night.

For some of us, it was also one of the few places that we could find jobs.

I was sixteen that summer, between my junior and senior years of high school.

Pirate Pete's meandered through oak trees dripping with Spanish moss. Even though it wasn't near the actual ocean, there was an algae-choked manmade lagoon where you could play water bumper-cars or climb around on a small replica pirate ship (mostly made of fiberglass) moored at the dock.

There was a pirate-themed mini-putt course, game booths, high seas merchandise booths, a couple of rickety kiddie rides, and a snack shack run by a guy who slept there at night. I have no idea where he went after the park closed in September. Maybe he lived there year round.

I worked one of the game booths. Cannons instead of guns that shot a stream of water, and you tried to knock over flat pirate ships instead of ducks or whatever. Arrrgh, and all that. The easiest thing to win was a black eye patch, which the little kids loved. You worked your way up through a red polyester sash, a plastic sword, a pirate hat…. Win them all and you had all the accouterments of a proper scourge of the seven seas.

It was a shitty place to work in many ways. Pirate Pete— yes, the place was owned and run by a guy named Pete, or if he had any other name, I never knew it—nickel-and-dimed his employees any way he could. Because it was a seasonal job, he didn't have to pay us minimum wage. We had to wear official Pirate Pete's T-shirts, which we had to purchase ourselves (and in the heat and humidity of the Florida Heartland, you had to have at least two, depending on how often your mother was willing to do your laundry). If you wanted water from the snack shake, you had to pay for the cup. *Lame.*

The later it got in the season, the less easy it became to win the bigger prizes at the game booths, because Pete didn't want to pay to restock. So in my booth, one of the ships would be nearly impossible to knock over, or the required number of ships you had to knock over got higher as the summer wore on, I was told.

Looking back, I'm amazed nobody got food poisoning or worse from the food at the snack shack (I had the misfortune of being back by the grill once, and it was horrifying, but there was nowhere else to get food, so I sucked it up like everyone else), or needed a tetanus shot after clambering around the creaky old ship. Maybe it was the time, or the fact that there wasn't much else to do, but nobody seemed to worry or complain.

On the other hand, Pete tended to turn a blind eye to certain items and activities. As long as things didn't get too out of hand, he never said a word about alcohol hidden in flasks or Coke bottles, cigarettes that stank more like skunk than tobacco, or some hanky-panky in a dark corner of the ship.

One thing I'll say for Pete: he had zero tolerance for anyone harassing women, especially his female employees. It was as if he had eyes in the back of his head when it came to that. One night I was working the cannon game and a couple of drunk guys in their early twenties were more interested in *my* cannon balls, if you know what I mean, and the next thing I knew, Pete was right there, asking them to leave and kindly not return. I never saw him coming, had no idea he was anywhere nearby.

Pete himself was a character. He was somewhere between thirty and fifty, give or take, with acne-pocked skin that couldn't seem to grow anything more than a patchy beard. Lanky, too-long brown hair, sharp dark eyes. He was of middling height, lean in a way that spoke of hunger or drugs or both, and he had a mild limp. When he put on the pirate costume, you could imagine him on a ship.

Not as the captain, though. As a hungover, hardened swabbie, sure.

At least he had all his teeth, tobacco-stained as they were.

Some of the other girls thought he was creepy, and in some ways he was, plus there was the whole skinflint thing—but I knew he looked out for us girls, and that gave him a leg up in my book.

ABOUT A MONTH INTO THE SUMMER, I WAS LEAVING AFTER closing one night when I realized I needed to get my extra clean shirt from my locker to wear the next day. Today had been especially humid—like walking through thick, hot mist—and the one I had at home hadn't been washed yet. Some of us were planning to drive around for a while tonight, and I didn't want to get up early to do laundry tomorrow.

I left Kathy, Tony, Stacie, and Brian at the car in the dirt parking lot, where we'd been hanging out for the last fifteen minutes or so, sitting on the hood or leaning on the side, listening to the new tape by The Police.

I walked down the path to the front entrance, the sound of voices and "Synchronicity II" fading behind me, replaced by the faint chorus of frogs from the lagoon. It was dim, just a few lights along the ground to lead me through the tunnel of oaks to the front gate, a wooden structure shaped and painted like a pirate ship, with openings all along and plank walkways leading into them. There were no doors; there was a gate at the end of the parking lot that was locked at night.

Inside, I headed straight, between rows of souvenir booths to entice you to buy a hat or sword on your way in to enhance your experience, or a shirt or plastic cup with a Pirate Pete's logo on your way out. When I got to the central courtyard, I'd turn left towards the snack shack and beyond it, the low building that served as the office and employee break room.

I didn't get that far.

In my defense, we'd been passing around rum and Diet Coke in the parking lot, so while I wasn't drunk by any stretch, I certainly wasn't at my sharpest.

The tall, streetlamp-like lights shaped like lanterns had been turned off, leaving only the ground lights and a few security lights on here and there. I heard them before I saw them, but by that time it was too late.

Pete, and two men. Pete still had on his black pirate pants and flowing white shirt and black boots, but had taken off his vest and sash and hat. Now he looked like an extra in a bad music video.

The two men facing him wore black pants and shirts. Both had dark hair, cut short, and both were more muscular than Pete. One was taller, one was about the same height as Pete.

The taller one had a gun. He wasn't pointing it at Pete, but it was there in his hand, a dull gleam in the knee-high light.

I stopped dead in my tracks, but it was too late. I saw Pete glance at me, shake his head fiercely, then heard a murmur as he said something to the men.

The tall man gestured at me with the gun. "Girl," he said. "Come here."

Pete closed his eyes, shook his head again, this time a small, defeated gesture.

Even in my haze, I knew running would be a stupid idea. Especially in my haze. I walked over to them. As I did, the men shifted so the light was behind them, making it harder to see their faces.

A black duffel bag sat on the ground between them and Pete.

"Gina," Pete said. "What the hell are you doing here?"

"I forgot my shirt," I said. Oh, so lame. I thought of my parents, trusting me to get home safely. Happy that I'd found a job, even one that didn't pay much. Proud that I was doing well in school, that I was headed to college.

"What did you hear?" the tall man asked.

"Nothing," I said, which was the god's honest truth. I'd heard voices, but murmurs, not words. My shirt stuck to my suddenly sweaty skin. It had been over ninety today, and until now, the low seventies of the evening had felt cool. "I swear."

I couldn't look at his eyes. I found myself focusing on his thin lips.

"Have her get the cash," suggested the short man.

I looked at Pete. He was shaking. Now I was really scared.

"Gina," Pete said. "I'm sorry. You know the storage closet in the office?"

I nodded.

"The shelf of extra coffee. Go get the last can on the left in the back. Can you do that?"

I nodded again.

He fumbled in his pocket, and the other two men tensed, but Pete brought out a ring of keys. It took him several tries to find the right one and hand the ring to me, that key facing up.

"Don't take too long, girl," the tall man said. I didn't feel tipsy anymore, just nauseated. I understood the threat in what he said.

I walked fast down the left path, skirted the snack shack. My hands trembled when I tried to unlock the door to the office and I nearly dropped the keys twice. Finally the knob turned, and I stumbled in, fumbling for the switch on the wall.

I blinked in the sudden brightness, and the first thing my eyes focused on was the black phone sitting on the desk.

I could call the police. Lock the door and hope bullets couldn't pierce the thin walls.

But I'd gotten a glance at the unzipped duffel bag at their feet, and seen the white bricks smothered in plastic wrap.

If I called the cops, Pete was going down, too.

More importantly, Pirate Pete might not have been the best employer ever, or even the best person ever, but I wasn't going to be responsible for him getting shot.

Or me, either.

I located the Chock Full o'Nuts cans on the closet shelves, and pulled out the one Pete had asked for.

It wasn't as heavy as the others. I couldn't help myself. I peeled back the white plastic lid.

Should I have been surprised by the roll of hundreds? Probably not. I still sucked in my breath at the sight of all that money.

Hastily I replaced the lid, shut off the light, slammed the door behind me. I wasn't going to waste time locking back up. If Pete was gonna fire me for that, fine.

I jogged back to the courtyard. As I approached, all three men turned to watch me. I stumbled, caught myself. When I got to them, I handed the can to Pete. The two men stank of cloying aftershave, and Pete smelled like sweat. I probably did, too. I felt sweaty and gross.

"Can she go?" Pete asked.

"Hang on," tall guy said. "Show me."

Just as I had done, Pete peeled back the lid.

Tall guy looked at me. I still couldn't—wouldn't—meet his gaze.

"Don't think about telling anyone," he said. "Your prints are all over this can."

The rest of me might have been dripping, but my mouth was dry. I worked up some saliva. "Okay." I sucked in a breath. "Can I go?"

He gestured with the gun, and I turned and ran until I was outside the stupid pirate ship gate. Then I slowed down, swallowing against the bile burning in my throat. As I got closer to the parking lot, I could hear voices and music. They'd changed cassettes to Van Halen.

Tony looked at me curiously when I got back to the car, his blue eyes wide. "You okay?"

"I'm not feeling well," I said. "Can you take me home?" I

grabbed the bottle of rum and Coke, took a swig. It wasn't what I wanted, but it was liquid.

To his credit, he did, without question. Stacie put her arm around me as he drove.

I didn't sleep much that night.

THE NEXT MORNING, I DID LAUNDRY, THEN GOT ON MY bike and pedaled to Pirate Pete's. The parking lot gate was locked, but there was ample space between the metal post on the left and the oak tree to squeeze a body and a bike through. I got there before the park opened.

I have to admit I felt a sense of relief when I barged into the office and Pete was there, alive.

"Gina," he said. "I didn't expect…"

"This is my, um, notice." I thrust the clean shirts at him.

He stared at them for a long moment, then took them and set them on the dented, gun-metal-grey desk.

"It's okay," he said. "I was going to suggest you go, or let you go, anyway."

I didn't know what to say.

"Hang on." Pete got up, went to the supply closet. He came back, and said, "Here are your wages, as well as a refund for the shirts."

He counted bills into my hand, faster than I could keep up, although I could tell it was more than he owed me.

"Thank you," I said when he finished, and stuffed the bills in my pocket.

"You're a good kid, Gina," he said. "I'm sorry about last night, I really am. I hope you have a good life."

I WAS LUCKY. A NEW CHAIN, HARDEE'S, BOUGHT OUT OUR Burger Chef, and I managed to snag a job for the rest of the summer. What it lacked in ambiance, it made up for in perks. Such as minimum wage and free soft drinks. The orange polyester top and paper hat were ugly, but at least I didn't have to pay for them. And blessed air conditioning.

When I worked the evening shift, my friends hung out there near closing, sucking on ketchup-drenched fries until I was free. Although several of them ditched Pirate Pete's over the course of the summer, they never asked about that night. And I was grateful.

AFTER THE SUMMER, HARDEE'S LET ME WORK WEEKENDS during the school year, and I was back on full time for the summer after my senior year until I went to Florida State in the fall.

The A/C was almost too cold, and dry. I'd been drinking more water than soda.

It was a slow mid-week afternoon, halfway between the lunch and dinner rushes. I heard the door open, but finished stuffing napkins into a plastic dispenser before I looked up. "Welcome to Hardee's, may I take your order."

Then I focused on him. Same pockmarked face, same intense brown eyes. His raggedy hair had been cut short, though, and he was wearing jeans and a Camel cigarettes T-shirt.

He stood still for a moment. "Gina."

I wore a nametag, but I knew he hadn't looked at it, that he had seen me.

"Hey, Pete. How...how are you?"

"Hanging in there. You doing okay?"

"I am. Heading to FSU in the fall."

"Good," he said, with more emotion than I expected. My heart squeezed. "Good for you."

He slid a twenty across the counter to me but didn't order anything. He just turned and walked out.

I don't know why I was sad to see him go.

SOMETIME AFTER THAT, AFTER I'D GRADUATED FROM college, Pirate Pete's shut down. I don't know whether it was because of health and safety crackdown, the emergence of videogame arcades and Chuck E. Cheese franchises in the area, or the drug deals that had probably been keeping the place alive.

I never saw Pirate Pete again.

I hoped he found another job.

I hoped he was safe.

THE SCENT OF AMBER AND VANILLA

mber and vanilla still haunted my dreams.

Amber and vanilla were the combined scents Chrissy always wore—still wore, no doubt, if they allow perfume in the psych ward. At first I thought they were sweet, just as I thought she was sweet, all blond and curvy and femme.

Sweet smells can't mask the underlying rot forever, though.

Now, sometimes I thought I smelled those cloying scents in the house, and my heart would race, and if my toddler daughter was home I'd run to her room to make sure she was safe.

I still woke up in a panic now, ripping the sleep mask from my face because for once I'd had a few free hours to myself, lay down and, to my surprise, actually napped. I didn't sleep well anymore, thanks to Chrissy.

The afternoon summer sun slanted through the blinds, striping the faded crazy quilt on the double bed and the wall opposite the window, where I'd hung one of my pieces of art.

A photograph of Taylor, my daughter, when she was a baby, collaged with pictures of my parents and siblings as babies.

I sat up, took a deep breath. Taylor was safe at a birthday party—Shannon, the birthday girl's mom, had said they had enough adults there to cover all the 3-year-olds, so I'd come back home for a couple of hours of rare *me* time.

Taylor was safe, I repeated to myself. The imagined odor of amber and vanilla faded. I glanced at the clock. Crap! I'd slept longer than expected—the party was due to end in five minutes, and it was fifteen minutes across town. I threw my clothes back on—jeans and a T-shirt which, with sneakers, constituted your basic harried single mom of a toddler outfit —and dashed to the bathroom to splash water on my face.

I grabbed my phone as I slipped on my sneakers, hit Shannon's number.

"Hi, it's Melody, I'm going to be a couple minutes late picking Taylor up, I'm on my way now—"

"Sweetie, your girlfriend already picked her up."

My blood slowed as it froze in my veins, time slowing along with it. The world closed in, darkness at the edge of my vision, until all that existed was the terror.

I hadn't told anyone that Chrissy had gone crazy, had nearly killed me, had nearly killed Taylor. It was hard enough living in a small town without facing that kind of scrutiny. Most people didn't believe lesbian partner abuse existed, especially not when neither party was particularly butch. And Chrissy had been very, very good at putting on the sweet face in front of everyone. She fooled even me, at the beginning.

Which is why it had taken so long for me to convince the police that there was a problem. Why it had to escalate to a knife at Taylor's throat for them to take me seriously.

"Melody? Are you there?" Shannon asked.

I had to force words out. "Hi, sorry. You said Chrissy

picked her up?" My voice wobbled, adrenaline spiking through it. "Did she say where they were going?"

"Nope." I heard a faint crash in the background, and Shannon yelled, away from the phone, "Madison! What the —" She came back. "Gotta go. Madison just decided to pull the leftover cake down on her head."

I shoved the phone in my pocket as I yanked my bedroom door open.

Then the wave of aroma hit me.

Amber and vanilla.

Jesus fucking Christ, Chrissy *was* here. *In the house.*

I didn't have a gun in the house—not ever, especially not with a small child—and I cast about for something, anything, I could use to defend myself and Taylor. Since Chrissy, I'd taken some self-defense classes, but I needed more than my bare hands.

Although if she hurt my sweet baby girl, bare hands were all it was going to take.

I couldn't afford a big place, so my drafting table and art supplies were squeezed into a corner of my bedroom. I grabbed an X-Acto knife out of the jumble of brushes and pens. Not a hefty plastic one like a box cutter, but the size of a pencil, made of rough, cold metal for better grip.

I slid out the small razor blade. It wasn't much—the size of my pinkie nail, useful only for fine detail work—but it was sharp. It was better than nothing.

I thumbed my phone on, typed in 911, but hesitated before I hit Send. I didn't know what I was going to find downstairs.

If Chrissy had a knife to Taylor's throat again, sirens could send her over the edge.

I went down the stairs quietly, my sneakers silent on the ugly tan carpet I could never find the money to replace, skipping the step that squeaked, which I'd always joked would trip up Taylor the first time she'd try to sneak in after curfew when she was a teenager.

I swore to myself now that she'd make it to teenager-hood.

Stealth didn't make a difference. When I stepped slowly into the living room, the full force of the sweet perfume hit me and there was Chrissy, kicked back on the sofa as if she still lived here, paging through an old *Entertainment Weekly* I'd brought home from work. She looked up, smiled.

To anyone else, it would have been a brilliant, pretty smile.

But I could see that it didn't reach her thick-lashed blue eyes; that her teeth looked ever so slightly bared.

I palmed the X-Acto knife, hiding my hand slightly behind me so she wouldn't see it.

Her hair was cropped short, but instead of making her look masculine, it gave her an even more innocent, gamine air. She wore a blue tank top and normal grey sweatpants. Where they standard issue at the psych ward? Or had she bought them somehow? And how had she gotten here? Where had she gotten money?

I'd changed the bank accounts, of course—hell, I'd changed banks just to be safe.

I probably should have left town, left the Northeast entirely, taken Taylor and gone somewhere anonymous like the Midwest, or lost myself in the overcrowded wackiness of Los Angeles or San Francisco. But I'd stayed, tried to keep life normal for Taylor (who, with the innocence of a 3-year-old, had somehow come through the whole ordeal without any lingering trauma). Here was normal, even if I didn't have a lot of close friends. I had my physiotherapy job at the hospital, I had the house—which of course I owed more on than I could sell it for, another reason to stay, even if the place wasn't anything to write home about.

I just hadn't thought Chrissy would ever get out. The police and her psychiatrist had assured me that she was clearly a danger to others.

So many questions, so many fears.

"Where's Taylor?" I demanded.

Chrissy stood, still smiling. She barely came up to my shoulder, but I knew how strong she was, and quick.

And completely batshit unpredictable.

"Is that any way to welcome home your lover?" she asked.

"Where is my daughter?"

Her smile faded. "Goddammit, Melody, that's all you ever think about. Don't worry, she's fine. She's safe where she is."

"And where is that?" I tightened my grip on the X-Acto knife.

"I'm not going to tell you that," she said. "We're going to talk, and you're going to apologize, and when everything is all better between us, we'll go get Taylor and be a family again." She didn't even try to smile. "Otherwise, you'll never see your precious rugrat again."

Family. It was what I'd always wanted, ever since I was a kid surrounded by sisters and brothers. Even when I came out, I'd known I'd wanted children. I'd already been doing fertility treatments when I met Chrissy, and she'd stood by me during the pregnancy and birth, never hinting that she didn't like kids, didn't want them...or whatever it was she felt.

All I knew was that everything had seemed fine while Taylor was a baby, but when she'd turned 3, something changed in Chrissy.

Subtle things at first: "forgetting" to keep an eye on Taylor when she played in the plastic kiddie pool in the backyard or they were at the mall. Accidentally dropping things on her—although I'd managed to snatch Taylor out of the way when Chrissy lost her grip on a pot of boiling water. Then escalating: I found little bruises on Taylor, and she stopped wanting to be alone with Mama Chrissy.

But Taylor was just a toddler, still babbling about her stuffies talking to her, still believing that Dora the Explorer was real. So I believed Chrissy when Taylor's version was that Chrissy had pushed her out of the car and Chrissy's version was that Taylor had undone her car seat (which I knew she could do, damn those surprisingly dexterous chubby fingers) and opened the door and fallen, and thank goodness they hadn't been going very fast.

In hindsight, I can't believe I was so blind.

And yet, Chrissy had told me that her only sibling, her younger sister, had died when she was 3, and somehow I got it into my head that she was projecting some kind of fear.

But then I caught Chrissy pinching Taylor, hard. It wasn't abuse as in beating her for doing something wrong. It was more...wanting to hurt her. When I confronted her, I saw—truly saw, for the first time—the nasty expression that flitted ever so quickly across her face.

From there, it had only gotten worse, and fast. Slamming Taylor's fingers in the car door (that time, I believed Taylor). Mixing bleach with the apple juice in Taylor's favorite Donald Duck sippy cup (I'd smelled it before Taylor drank any, and Chrissy insisted it must've been left over from when we did the dishes, but I never, ever let her near Taylor's food again). I filed police reports, and Chrissy sweet-talked the cops.

Until the knife. Her ranting and raving, me dialing 911, her letting Taylor go when the doorbell rang and her face changing into a friendly smile as she greeted the officers.

But I'd installed a nanny cam, and the footage finally convinced them.

I took a deep breath, trying to remember everything my therapist had told me about finding my inner calm place. It didn't work. My skin felt as though it was going to fly off of me, and the adrenaline was making everything loud and immediate.

"You want us to be a family again," I said. I knew she'd never tell me where Taylor was unless I played along, even if she wasn't making any sense. If she truly wanted us to be a family, she wouldn't've just referred to Taylor as my precious rugrat, not in that acid-dripping tone. "Okay. Fine. Let's talk."

She walked towards me then, came up close, and it was all I could do not to flinch.

"First," she said, "give me the phone."

Dammit. My stomach twisted as I handed it to her—the screen had gone dark; I'd missed my chance to call 911—using the motion to hide the action of sliding the X-Acto blade back into the sheath and tucking the knife in my back pocket. There was no telling what she would do if she saw me holding it.

She tossed the phone on the coffee table without a glance.

Then she held out her arms and tilted her head up and said, "Give us a kiss," and it was all I could do not to plunge the tiny blade into her, all my fear and terror behind it.

Dimly, I knew that wasn't like me. I wasn't a violent person. But I'd read all the studies about mothers protecting their children, and I understood where this raging impulse was coming from.

Saving my daughter was forefront in my mind, and would be until she was safely in my arms again.

So I kissed Chrissy, faking passion, and thankfully she didn't press the issue further. She took my hand, again all smiling and seemingly happy, and led me to the sofa. The amber and vanilla was suffocating.

"You've changed things around," she said, looking at the mantle. Her mouth turned down at the corners. "Where's all our stuff, everything the two of us built together?"

"I packed it up," I lied. The framed photos, the faded silk

rose I'd won for her at the county fair, the shells we'd picked up on the beach the one time we'd gone to Maine after an unexpected tax return—I'd thrown it all out, shuddering.

But I couldn't tell her that. I frantically improvised. "It was too hard to look at it when...when you went away," I said. "I thought I'd bring it back out once you were home again."

"I didn't like being away. I didn't like it there," she said.

"I know," I said, as soothingly as I could manage. "But you know you were...stressed, and sometimes it's best to get away for a little while to decompress."

"It wasn't a fucking spa," she snapped, and I did flinch, just a little.

I didn't know how to do this. I'd talked to a therapist, I'd read books, but I was not an expert in unpredictable crazy people or hostage negotiation. I felt a sob rising up, pushed it back. No matter what I said, Chrissy was going to get mad.

And I'd never see Taylor again.

If Taylor was even alive.

"I'm sorry," I said. "Maybe I made a mistake, sending you there. I only wanted what was best for you."

"What else are you sorry for?" she asked.

I blinked, thinking furiously. What did she want me to be sorry for?

"For not trusting you," I said. "I do want us to be a family again, Chrissy—just like you do. You and me and Taylor—"

"Goddammit!" Chrissy shot to her feet, nearly tripping over the walnut veneer coffee table. "That's not what I want! I want things to go back to back to the way they were!"

"Honey," I soothed, tugging at her sweatpants, trying to bring her back down. "That's what I was saying: back to the way things were before you went away."

Chrissy didn't sit down. She walked over to the wall, to a picture I'd painted of Whiteface Mountain covered in snow. She poked at the frame, making the picture swing back and forth. "That's not what I meant," she said, her voice almost petulant. "That's not what a family is."

She wasn't making sense. What was I supposed to do, dammit?

"Then let's figure out what a family is," I said. "You tell me."

"It's like..." She shook her head. "It's like, before Patty."

My first thought was that she'd meant "before Taylor." But then I remembered: Patty had been her baby sister. The one who'd died at age 3, when Chrissy was 8.

Maybe I'd had this all wrong. She'd never wanted to talk about Patty, so I didn't know the details and had never pushed her. Maybe she was scared that now that Taylor was the same age as Patty, that Taylor was going to die, too?

It didn't line up with her actions, but who knew what was logical to her?

I had to get my hands on my phone, call 911. If she saw me doing that, I was sure she'd go apeshit. But if I grabbed the phone and left her alone while I called, she might leave, might go hurt Taylor.

Might kill Taylor.

I had to believe that Taylor was still alive.

"I think I understand," I said. "I don't know what happened to Patty, but I promise you, I won't let the same thing happen to Taylor. Taylor won't die."

"It was all fine until *she* came along!" Chrissy shouted. She whirled, her arm flashed out, and she swept everything off the mantle—a portrait of Taylor, a vase of wilting black-eyed Susans we'd picked up on a walk, an unidentifiable *thing* Taylor had made out of Popsicle sticks at day care and presented to me with so much pride I hadn't the heart to question its raison d'être.

The vase shattered, water that should have been changed

two days ago splashing up the wall. I couldn't stop a small shriek of fear at the violent sound.

"It was just Mom and me, and we were happy, and when Patty came Mom had to work and I helped take of Patty and Mom told me she loved me and hugged me when Patty was asleep." Chrissy's words were coming out almost faster than I could follow them. "But then Mom didn't have to work anymore and she took care of Patty and Patty didn't need me anymore and Mom was too busy with Patty to love me." She looked at me, her eyes focusing on me as if she'd forgotten I was there.

"Chrissy," I said carefully. "What happened to Patty?"

Chrissy's chin came up. "It was an accident. That's what everyone said."

Oh. *Shit*.

I understood, with terrifying clarity, that it hadn't been an accident. Chrissy must have killed Patty, and then Taylor had turned the same age and now she was a threat, too, getting between Chrissy and I just as she'd perceived Patty got in the way between herself and her mother.

I still had the X-Acto knife, but it wasn't going to be enough. My eyes fell on the remains of the mantle decorations, broken and scattered on the floor next to the fireplace.

I'd wired shut the doors of the brass 1970s fireplace screen so Taylor couldn't crawl in there as a baby, and I'd never reopened it, but the set of tools—brush, ash shovel, and poker—still sat next to it.

Weapons.

But Taylor was out there somewhere and only Chrissy knew where, and I didn't think threatening Chrissy would do any good.

I had a feeling she'd rather die than reunite me with my daughter.

"Chrissy," I said. Once last chance to get through to her.

"I won't let that happen with Taylor. You and I are always going to be solid, always a team. Taylor's not going to come between us. Look, we'll find a sitter, go on date nights, take weekends away—make sure we're connecting, just you and me.

"I..." It was almost impossible to choke the words out, make them sincere. "I love you."

It might have worked. It might have been enough to convince her to take me to Taylor. I'd never know, though, because at that moment my phone rang, and the name that flashed up was psychiatric facility Chrissy had escaped from.

About fucking time, you think?

Except it set Chrissy off like nothing else had.

With a wordless shriek of rage, she snatched the phone off the coffee table and threw it onto the floor. When it didn't break against the carpeting, she stomped down on it. The screen cracked audibly, and the ringing stopped.

She ground it into the carpet with her heel, stomped again, then once more, her expression a combination of rage and derangement.

I noticed—a stupid detail at a time like this—that she wore those socks with rubber grips on the bottom. Was that what they had to wear at the loony bin? She must not have been able to find shoes in her size quickly.

"Fuck this! *Fuck this!*" she screamed.

She dashed for the door, and I dashed for the fireplace poker. But as she yanked open the door, she grabbed my keys out of the basket on the small table next to the door. I'd always kept them there, so of course she knew they'd be there.

Then she was outside, and with an arm practiced from her women's softball league, flung my keys. They arced and glinted in the sunlight, and landed in the overgrown field next door.

She ran to a car at the curb, and I ran after her, but I hesitated before I swung that poker, because if I stopped her, I'd never find Taylor alive.

Tires squealed as she peeled away. I dashed into the field, scrabbling at the shin-high weeds. Dandelion puffs danced in the air (Taylor treated dandelion puffs as if they were the most miraculous things on earth).

Where...where, dammit?

There!

I snatched them up, but then I ran back inside. I didn't know where she'd gone, but I'd memorized the license of her car, knew the color and style (I didn't know cars well enough to ID make and model, but it had two doors). Then I remembered: no phone. I grabbed it anyway, shoved it back in my pocket.

Think. I had to think. The keys jangled in my shaking hands. Where would she go? Where would she hide Taylor? Could she have rented a motel room? Or a storage unit?

My gut said no. My gut said she was going to fixate on something, go somewhere familiar or meaningful.

I stared at the pile of stuff on the floor, at the mantle that Chrissy had gazed at, demanding to know where our things had gone. I tried to remember what I'd previously tried so hard to forget: What had been up there before? The rose from the fair and the shells from Maine—but the fair was months away and Maine was 300 miles away.

There had been photos, too. Photos of... I closed my eyes, visualizing.

The largest photo, the one that had been front and center.

Chrissy and I, at the mini-putt place off Route 22. The Enchanted Land. It was where we'd gone on our first date, and where we'd had our their first kiss (kissing in public, no less, and for the first time I hadn't cared who saw us, hadn't cared if we'd be judged, because nothing had existed but the two of us), and where I'd asked her to move in with me, the most commitment we could legally make at the time.

As the memories flooded in, I headed to my car.

We'd stopped going to the Land of Enchantment when my pregnant belly got in the way of my admittedly abysmal mini-golf swing, and then I'd been busy with the baby and work and life. I'd thought of it just before Taylor's third birthday, wondering if we should have her party there, but Chrissy said it had closed down.

She'd said, I remembered now, that it had been *our* place, anyway. I hadn't realized the depth of that statement until now.

The place had been abandoned after a new park opened by the public beach, complete with lazer tag and a go-kart track.

There were a hundred places around a desolate mini-putt course to hide a terrified 3-year-old.

My eyes teared up at the thought of Taylor, terrified and alone, and I didn't realize I'd shot through a stop sign until I heard horns blaring and tires screeching. Fuck it. As long as I didn't get pulled over.

I knew I should call the cops, but I didn't have time to stop and find a working phone. I had to get there and stop Chrissy before she hurt Taylor.

Before she killed my baby.

There weren't a lot of cars on the road, and I was speeding and hoping I'd catch up to Chrissy, because it was also possible I was wrong and she had Taylor stashed somewhere else. The highway had long, swooping curves, and because it was bordered on both sides by tall pines, it wasn't possible to see far ahead.

I had to believe I was right. My 8-year-old secondhand Accura coughed as I pushed it faster, but it didn't fail. The wipers might have a random idea of when to work and the radio might be busted except on blue moon Tuesdays when there were sunspots, but I poured whatever money I had (or barely had) into making sure the car drove and stopped properly, because I had a toddler to protect.

And now, a child to save.

A washed-out sign told me The Enchanted Land was a mile ahead on the right. As I rounded the next corner, I saw a car—it had to be Chrissy's—turn.

I got to the old entrance road, turned. My car bumped along the pitted dirt road, and then I was at the parking lot, tires crunching on the gravel. Chrissy's car was there, the front end against the chainlink fence as if she hadn't bothered to stop until she was forced to.

I scrambled out of my car. The padlock on the gate was broken. I shoved against it, squeezed through.

In front of me was a low, cement-block building that had held the ticket booth, room of ancient video games, and restaurant that had provided cheap hot dogs, lukewarm pizza, and soft-serve ice cream to kids whose blood sugar had dropped alarmingly while they'd been out the mini-putt course. On the wall was a large wooden arrow painted with the word Entrance; it listed down, now pointing forlornly at the ground.

I ran around to the doors, my feet hammering over more gravel. The glass had been broken out, as it had in the windows, all of it boarded over. Another chain and padlock served as a deterrent, as if there were anything left inside to steal.

Unless there were another way in, Chrissy and Taylor weren't inside.

I faced the mini-putt course. It was large, because the designers had worked hard on making the place all enchanted-y. Gingerbread houses, giant shoes for old ladies to live in, castles (at least one you could go into, if you were a kid or very short, and look down the stairs to a dungeon that held a glowing red dragon), and other fairy-tale-related objects were scattered about.

For a kid, it was a magical wonderland. For teens and anyone else particularly horny, it provided a wealth of places to neck mostly unseen.

For me, it was a nightmare.

I ran to the first hole. I couldn't think of anywhere Chrissy would think of as particularly special. We'd never snuck into any place. I'd kissed her on the fifth hole as a defiant act, in some ways. Yes, we're queer. Deal with it. Nobody had noticed, or cared.

Where, where?

Then I noticed, on the torn, faded faux grass of the putting channel, something red and glistening.

Blood. A heel print of blood.

She must've cut her foot when she smashed my phone.

I followed the trail cross-country through the course, dodging unicorns and an empty pool presided over by a replica of the Little Mermaid statue in Copenhagen, and when I rounded a corner near the thirteenth hole, I saw Chrissy limping towards the big black witch's hat, as tall as me, that served as the "trap" you had to putt through.

I realized that somewhere—when I'd gone looking for the car keys? when I'd gotten out of the car?—that I'd dropped the fireplace poker.

A moment later, I saw a discarded mini-putt club in a half-dead decorative bush.

I grabbed it, and ran faster than I ever had.

Chrissy had been so intent on her path that she didn't hear me until I was nearly upon her. She turned, startled, one arm half-raised. I swung with all the fury of an enraged mother and slammed the little club into the side of her head.

She shrieked, fell. Didn't get up. I waited only a few seconds before I dropped to my knees before the archway into the witch's hat. It wasn't big enough for an adult to really squeeze into, but I could sort of wedge my shoulders through.

"Taylor! Tay-baby!"

She wasn't moving. Her wrists and ankles were bound with duct tape, another piece over her mouth (as if anyone would hear her out here). I dragged her towards me, ripped the tape off her face, pressed my fingers to her neck.

Heartbeat? Breath?

Her eyelids fluttered. "Mommy?"

I reached out to hug her. "Oh, baby." My eyes had barely adjusted to the dimness, but I could see how groggy she was. Chrissy, who'd worked as a medical assistant, must've known what to drug her with to keep her out.

A blaze of white-hot pain across my hips.

I pulled myself out of the small opening, twisting and throwing an arm up just as the club came down on my wrist. Pain flared there, but I scrabbled to my feet. Ducked, and the club bounced off the fiberglass of the hat.

I heard another noise, realized it was coming out of me, as I rose up and threw myself at Chrissy. Tackled her. Fell to the ground on top of her.

The club went skidding somewhere. She attacked with hands, fingers, nails. Surprisingly strong, she nearly flipped me over.

The toes of my sneakers skidded along the AstroTurf.

Somehow she got leverage. Crazy outweighed terror. Helpless, I rolled, and she was on top of me like a rabid wolverine.

Then I remembered the X-Acto knife in my back pocket.

My right hand was useless. In one final act of desperation, I thrust up with my hips, like a sick, twisted bout of lovemaking, jamming my left arm beneath me to reach my right pocket.

She straddled me, shoving my hips back down, and punched me.

I saw stars, floating like dandelion puffs.

I thrust up again, found the slim metal of the knife, yanked it free of my pocket.

"Mommy?" Or maybe it was the ringing in my ears.

I fumbled left-handed to push out the blade.

"We could've been a *family*," Chrissy said. Her hands went around my throat. I'd had no idea how terrifying that sensation was, of not being able to draw in air.

I couldn't see.

My thumb slid. I hoped that meant the blade was free.

Blindly, I lashed out.

Chrissy cursed.

I struck out again, and her hands left my throat.

I gulped in air, regained a little sight, slashed at her.

The tiny, razor-sharp blade caught her throat.

If she screamed, I didn't hear it. I felt hot liquid splash on my chest, and once again I shoved, and this time, she fell away.

I rolled over, struggled to my knees. Chrissy was making a horrible gurgling sound. I suppose I should've made sure she was dead, but she was down again, and I needed to get to Taylor.

By the time I tugged my baby out of the witch's hat, Chrissy was no longer making noise. I turned so I shielded the sight of her from Taylor, although Taylor was still clearly groggy.

My phone buzzed in my pocket, and it was my turn to shriek. I fished it out. Apparently it hadn't completely broken when Chrissy stomped on it.

I could see enough of the bottom of the screen to accept the call.

"Is this Melody Lacroix?"

"Yes. I need—"

"This is Doctor Justin Lashway of Clifton Psychiatric Hospital. I'm calling about Christine Morris."

"Yes, yes, I know." The phone nearly slipped through my blood-covered fingers. "I need police—an ambulance—to the old Land of Enchantment. I'm okay, I think Taylor's okay, but Chrissy..."

Jesus. What was I supposed to say?

"Call 911. Please."

I couldn't hold on to the phone anymore. It fell, almost silently, onto the AstroTurf of the thirteenth hole.

"Mommy?"

"You're safe," I crooned, cuddling Taylor against me. "You're safe. We're safe. We're okay."

The stench of blood wiped out the cloying scents of amber and vanilla.

We'd never have to smell that damn perfume again.

ABOUT THE AUTHOR

Dayle A. Dermatis is the author or coauthor of many novels (including snarky urban fantasies *Ghosted* and the forthcoming *Shaded* and *Spectered*) and more than a hundred short stories in multiple genres, appearing in such venues as *The Saturday Evening Post*, *Alfred Hitchcock's Mystery Magazine*, and DAW Books.

Called the mastermind behind the *Uncollected Anthology* project, she also guest edits anthologies for *Fiction River*, and her own short fiction has been lauded in many year's best anthologies in erotica, mystery, and horror.

She lives in a book- and cat-filled historic English-style cottage in the wild greenscapes of the Pacific Northwest. In her spare time she follows Styx around the country and travels the world, which inspires her writing.

To find out where she's wandered off to (and to get free fiction!), check out DayleDermatis.com and sign up for her newsletter or support her on Patreon.

I value honest feedback, and would love to hear your opinion in a review, if you're so inclined, on your favorite book retailer's site.

For more information:
www.dayledermatis.com

BE THE FIRST TO KNOW!

Sign up for Dayle A. Dermatis's newsletter for *free* fiction, plus the latest news, releases, and more.

Sign up at DayleDermatis.com.

For more in-depth conversations and special sneak peeks, you can also support her continued work by joining her community of patrons out Dayle's Patreon.

Patreon.com/Dayle